# LAST STAND!

Just as Anderson heard the first rush of an artillery shell, the VC made their assault. The woods were full of bugles, whistles, and shouts. The firing increased as the enemy surged from the trees.

Action erupted all along the line. M-16s and M-60s poured bullets into the attacking enemy. There were screams of hatred as the VC and NVA tried to overrun the American position.

Anderson tossed away his radio and turned to face the oncoming enemy. Using his M-16, he fired into the mass coming at him. He pulled the trigger twice and then flipped the selector to auto and began to fire four- and five-round bursts.

A single VC reached the aircraft and began to scramble over the tail boom. Anderson looked into the VC's dark, sweat-smeared face and pulled the trigger of his weapon. The enemy was lifted from his perch and tossed back, screaming.

But another took his place, firing down toward Anderson...

▼

## EAGLE EYE

## Also by Cat Branigan

*Wings Over Nam #1:*
*Chopper Pilot*

*Wings Over Nam #2:*
*The Wild Weasels*

*Wings Over Nam #3:*
*Linebacker*

*Wings Over Nam #4:*
*Carrier War*

*Wings Over Nam #5:*
*Bird Dog*

Published by
POPULAR LIBRARY

# WINGS OVER NAM #6

# EAGLE EYE

**POPULAR LIBRARY**

An Imprint of Warner Books, Inc

A Time Warner Company

POPULAR LIBRARY EDITION

Popular Library® and the fanciful P design are registered trademarks
of Warner Books, Inc.

Cover design by Jackie Merri Meyer/Richard J. Milano
Cover illustration by Cliff Miller

Popular Library books are published by
Warner Books, Inc.
666 Fifth Avenue
New York, N.Y. 10103

 A Time Warner Company

Printed in the United States of America

First Printing: November, 1990

10 9 8 7 6 5 4 3 2 1

# WINGS OVER NAM #3

## EAGLE EYE

# ONE

THE sudden flat bang and the falling dust woke him. David Alexander Anderson rolled from his bunk without thinking about it. He hit the dirty plywood floor, slipped right, under his cot, and then listened as the sirens around the perimeter and from the top of the control tower began to wail.

There was another crump as something detonated in the distance, but the sounds of the explosions were coming closer. Anderson rolled to the left, out from under his cot, and crawled to the doorway. As he reached it, there was another explosion closer to him and then a series of bangs that shook the hootch and rattled the tin roof. Dust filled the air, and there was the odor of fireworks.

Anderson leaped to his feet and sprinted down the short hallway. As he reached the door, there was a flash above him and an explosion that tossed him back, into the hootch. He hit the floor on his back, rolled, and pressed himself against the wall and the floor, trying to make himself as small as possible while covering his head with his hands.

The lights outside, tiny electric bulbs set on poles, flickered and died. Anderson was left in the dark, smelling the dust and the cordite. Through the open door he could make out the yawning shape of the entrance to the bunker, but he wasn't sure that he wanted to run to it—not with the mortars and rockets now falling on the company area with a regularity that suggested it was the target.

"You alive in there, Anderson?" yelled someone.

"Yeah."

"You hit?"

"No. I'm just waiting for the barrage to lift."

There was another detonation and shrapnel rattled off the roof. Anderson felt the concussion from the explosion. Dust drifted by the door, obscuring the bunker.

"Too close," yelled Anderson. "Coming out." He pushed himself up and ran for the door. He hurdled the boardwalk and dived for the bunker entrance, falling down the rough steps cut in the dirt.

The inside of the bunker smelled musty. There was a single bench down the center of it, and a couple of the men sitting there held flashlights. They were all young men now looking years older. Some wore fatigue pants and T-shirts, some were in their underwear, and a few wore combat boots. Two of them had on shower shoes. Anderson was surprised that anyone had on clothes. He'd jumped from his cot and was now sitting there in nothing more than his jockey shorts. The tropical humidity kept him from getting cold.

"You okay, sir?" asked Jordan. He was a crew chief who had flown with Anderson a couple of times.

Anderson scrambled around and sat down on the bench. He brushed at the dirt on his bare legs and chest and then nodded. "I'm fine."

The bunker had been dug between the hootches with a backhoe. It was a single trench, four feet wide, with perforated steel plate on the floor. The roof, also of PSP, was set up on fifty-five-gallon drums. Sandbags were stacked around the drums and on the PSP over them. There was a second set of drums, up on the PSP of the first, with another layer of sandbags and PSP. It was designed to detonate the rockets or mortar rounds. The shrapnel would be absorbed by the next layer, protecting the men sitting inside the bunker. Anderson had been told they could take a hit from a 122-millimeter rocket, but he wasn't sure. He knew that he didn't want to be in there when the theory was tested.

There was an explosion just outside the bunker. Dirt swirled in the air, and the men began to choke.

"Shit. Too close."

Anderson reached up to the first-aid kit stored near the door. "Anyone hurt?"

No one said a word. Anderson, holding the kit, glanced at the door. Outside, there was some distant shouting and the continuing wail of the mortar warning horn. It sounded like something taken from a 1965 Ford Fairlane.

Now it sounded as if the mortars were walking away from them. The detonations were duller, farther away. That was the thing about mortars. Anderson could tell if they were coming at him or moving away from him. With rockets, once they were launched, no one knew where they'd hit. Charlie aimed them at the biggest target and hoped for the best.

The lights flickered and came on in the bunker. They were hooked on a wire running along one side, out of the way. Anderson moved closer to the door and looked out. He still held the first-aid kit.

Now there were people running around—dark shapes and shadows—but there was no shooting. These were American soldiers searching for friends. Anderson pushed himself out of the bunker, but crouched in the doorway in case he needed to dive back inside.

A flickering fire burned to the right. Anderson stood up and watched as three men threw shovels of dirt into the flames.

"Anderson? You hurt?"

Anderson look at Captain Brown. "No, sir. I'm fine."

Brown nodded and pointed up at the roof of one of the hootches. There was a hole about three feet in diameter in the corrugated metal.

"Jesus."

"Lieutenant Hoskins. Doc's in with him now. Took some shrapnel."

Anderson was aware of others behind him. Now that the siren had stopped screaming, the men were coming up, out of the bunker. One of them stood there and asked, "How bad is it?"

Brown shrugged. "We've a couple of wounded and some damage to the company area."

Anderson glanced at him and then the other men. They were standing around like a bunch of civilians after a tornado had moved through. The danger might be over, but no one knew for sure. They were stunned, not believing that the enemy would actually drop mortar rounds on them or that the rounds would do damage. Fires burned, most of them small. There was debris scattered everywhere. Bits of wood and chunks of tin. Smoke, from the explosions and the fires, hung in the air. And the men milled around without direction. No one seemed to know what to do.

"Hey," yelled the doc. "Couple of you get in here and help me."

Anderson, still holding the first-aid kit, moved forward. He stopped at the door and looked inside. Unlike most of the other hootches, this one was one long, open bay. Three lieutenants lived in it. They had bought bamboo mats for the floor, and a couple of lawn chairs, and had built some furniture out of wooden ammo crates.

One of the men lay on his cot, blood staining his pillow and the single sheet. There were bandages on his throat and his shoulders. He was awake but not making a sound. His eyes were wide and white.

One of the other lieutenants was standing there telling everyone who would listen, "I thought he was right behind me. I didn't know he'd been hit. I thought he was right with me. I'd never have left him."

"I want to move the whole cot," said the doc. "Down to the dispensary. Once I get him there we can get an ambulance to take him up to the Twelfth Evac."

Anderson dropped the first-aid kit to the floor and walked around to grab the front of the cot. As he leaned down, the lieutenant looked up, right into his face. It looked as if the lieutenant was going to smile, and then as if he was going to be sick. He opened his mouth and blood poured out.

"Ah, shit!" said the doc.

He leaped forward, knelt next to the cot, and jerked the sheet down. There was a single small hole in the man's chest. There was a bubbly, bloody foam around the hole. The doc slapped his hand over the wound.

"Get on the horn and tell them we've got a badly wounded man. Someone get the ambulance up here." He looked at the men as they stood there, and screamed, "Move it. Now!"

Brown turned and ran from the hootch. A moment later there was the sound of a truck backing up, next to the boardwalk.

"Okay," said the doc. He moved his hand. There was no external bleeding. The wounded man had coughed, spitting blood on those near him, but was breathing normally again.

"Okay," said the doc again. "I want to move him to the ambulance. Carefully. There's some shrapnel in his chest and I don't want to jar it."

They lifted the cot, one man at each corner, with the doctor standing toward the front, his hand still pressed against the lieutenant's chest. For a moment they stood still, holding the cot, and then began maneuvering it toward the door. They stopped there, waited, and then turned, pushing their way through.

"Hold it," said one of the men. He stepped backward, trying to stay up on the board.

"Stop," said the doc. He let go and slipped through the door and then reached back, putting his hand on the wound. "Now, let's go."

The door was just wide enough for the cot. One man let go of his corner and stepped through and leaned back, taking the head of the cot, supporting it. Anderson then exited, and the two men at the far end came forward. They worked to hold the cot steady and level.

They maneuvered it through and then backed up. The company area was still dark, except for the firelight and a couple of dim bulbs. The man opposite Anderson slipped off the boardwalk. He let go of the cot and fell to his back. Anderson grabbed at the rail, holding on, steadying the cot.

"Jesus," said the man.

"You okay?" asked the doc.

The man stood up and brushed at himself. "Jesus. I'm fine. Fine."

They stopped for a moment. The ambulance had been backed up, and stood open. The driver held one of the doors. He said, "You'll never get that cot in here."

The doc looked at him. "Then unload the ambulance."

The driver stood silently for a moment and then began to push the stretchers around, making room for the cot.

"Doc!" yelled a man, running up from the right. "Doc. Crawford got hit."

"Where the hell is he?"

The man grinned. "In the shitter."

The doc looked at the man and asked, "He hurt bad?"

"No, but he stinks. Took some shrapnel is all. In the leg and right arm."

"Then get him in a jeep and get him up to the Twelfth Evac. I'll see him up there."

"Done." The man turned and ran off.

The driver stepped back, out of the way. Anderson carefully climbed up and into the rear of the ambulance. He leaned forward, trying to hold the cot level as the others pushed it in. When he reached the front of the ambulance and the cot was inside, he sat it down and moved around it.

The doc looked up. "Thanks."

The lieutenant who had been standing in the room saying that he didn't know anyone was left, pushed his way forward. "I'm going with him."

"No need for that," said the doc.

"I'm going."

"Climb in."

As he did, the driver shut the door and ran around to the front of the vehicle. He got in, slammed the door, opened it and slammed it again, and then roared off. Anderson watched the ambulance bounce through the company area and then out on the road that led to the Twelfth Evac.

As they stood there, the company commander, Major Fox, walked up. He said, "What happened here?"

"One of the new lieutenants took some shrapnel in the neck and chest," said Anderson.

"Which one?"

Anderson shrugged. "Hell, sir, all lieutenants look the same to me. One of the new ones. I don't know his name."

"Hell of a note. Man gets wounded and no one knows his name," said Fox.

Anderson was about to say something flip in return, but decided against it. Instead he asked, "How badly did we get hurt tonight?"

"Not too bad. Five wounded that I know of. No one killed. Some damage to the hootches. Supply took a hit, but I think most of the shrapnel was absorbed by clothes. No equipment."

There was the sound of a helicopter winding up across the street, in the revetments. "Counter mortar," said Fox unnecessarily.

"Getting off a little late aren't they?"

Fox shot Anderson a glance. "You want to run for the revetments during a mortar attack?"

"No, sir. Just saying that it seems to be a little late for it now."

Fox nodded. "Hell, the tower crew might have seen

something, or some of the men on the bunker line. Give our people a direction to fly for the search.''

"Should be a better way to do that.''

There was a sudden explosion, but none of the men standing around even ducked. It was all outgoing. The artillery on the northern side of the camp was now firing in response to the Vietcong mortar and rocket attack. It too was a little late to be effective.

"Shit,'' said Anderson. "Like pissing in a forest fire. Not going to do a hell of a lot of good.''

"Let's Charlie know that we're out and about and still alive,'' said Fox. "Even if it doesn't put out the fire, it gives us something to do.''

"Yes, sir,'' said Anderson.

# TWO

ANDERSON was sitting in the mess hall drinking coffee and wishing that the club was open so that he could get a Coke instead. Hot coffee in the tropics just didn't do it for him—especially when the coffee was so bad that he had to fill it with sugar to make it palatable. He knew that later he would have to drink a gallon of water to eliminate the effects of the sugar.

The mess hall was a cross-shaped building with the kitchen in the center of it. Officers had one selection, NCOs another, and the enlisted men the final two. The walls were made of sections of plywood about four feet tall, with screen the rest of the way up. There were ceiling fans hung from the rafters and two large fans roaring at each end in an attempt to circulate the air.

Sitting with Anderson were Thomas Nichols and Bill

Craig. Nichols was a young man with the beginnings of a blond mustache. He had light hair, a badly sunburned face, and fine features. Although he had been in Vietnam for nine months, he had yet to acquire a tropical tan. It looked as if he'd arrived no more than a day or two earlier.

Craig was also young, but where Nichols was tall and slim, Craig was short and stocky. He had black hair and brown eyes and a deep tan. The mustache that he had started a week earlier was already thick. It looked as if he had been working on it for a couple of months.

Both men looked tired. Both wore sweat-stained, wrinkled fatigues, and Craig had a smudge of grease on his forehead. He sat with his hands wrapped around the coffee cup as if afraid that the heat would escape. He stared down into it, ignoring everything that was going on around him.

Anderson pushed his cup away and then looked down at the metal tray sitting in front of him holding pale yellow scrambled eggs, dark brown hash browns, and a couple of slices of limp toast. He decided that he didn't want to eat breakfast. He didn't want to do anything.

No one spoke for a moment, and then Nichols shook his head. "It's just a waste of time."

"What's a waste of time?"

"Counter-mortar. By the time we can get airborne, Charlie has beat feet. Rockets are even worse. Charlie doesn't even have to be there. Aim them during the day, set some kind of timer, and then slip away." Nichols had flown the unsuccessful counter-mortar mission Anderson had seen lift off after the previous night's attack.

"Then there's no way to catch him," said Anderson.

"If we patrolled during the day we might see him

slipping in. Hell, put enough people in the sky and Charlie won't be able to move. It's the secret of the war."

Anderson laughed. "I'm going to have to start writing this stuff down. Secret of the War Number Twenty-seven. Put enough people in the sky."

"You know what I mean," said Nichols.

"Sure, but if we fought this thing the way we should, it would have been over before you or I had graduated from high school, let alone got through flight school."

"And it's the only war we've got," said Craig, speaking for the first time.

Anderson shot him a glance and then shook his head. He shoved the tray of food away violently and said, "This whole thing is making me sick."

"How so?"

"Oh, hell, think about it. The Chairborne Commandos in Saigon like to say that the night belongs to Charlie. But why? If Charlie moves through the night, shouldn't we be out there in the night looking for him? Charlie lays low during the day while we're in the field. We call it off at dusk and Charlie begins to move. What bullshit."

"So you're willing to fly at night. In the dark," said Nichols.

"Hell, you were out there last night, flying in the dark. Besides, it'll be harder to see us at night. We won't be the big fat targets we are now."

"Man's got a point," said Craig. "Man's got a point."

"So what are you going to do about it?" asked Nichols.

Anderson gestured at his collar where the subdued warrant officer's bar was sown. "I don't have the power to do anything. No one listens to wobbly ones. Hell, they won't listen unless I'm a colonel, and if I'm a colonel, I'm just getting my ticket punched. I don't want to make waves, so I keep my mouth shut, spend my year, and go home covered in glory.''

''Then this whole conversation is bullshit,'' said Nichols.

''At least I know what the fuck I'm talking about,'' said Anderson. ''You think about it, you'll see that I'm right. Hell, I'm the lowest-ranking officer, a technician, granted the warrant only so that the army can feel good about my flying helicopters, but even I can see the flaw in the army's plan. You don't defeat the enemy by going where he isn't. You search him out and destroy him, and if you have to do it at night, that's when you do it.''

''Thank you for that analysis, General Patton,'' said Nichols sarcastically.

Anderson laughed. ''You may crack wise here, but you know I'm right.''

The loudspeaker went off then. ''Attention in the company area. Attention in the company area. Scramble all flight crews. I say again. Scramble all flight crews. ACs report to operations now.''

Anderson shoved back his chair and stood up. As he turned, he noticed a couple of the other pilots in the chow line. They left their trays sitting in front of the serving area. One man who had just stepped in pointed to his name on the roster and then shook his head. He wouldn't be eating the meal and therefore shouldn't have to pay for it.

Anderson walked out of the mess hall and down the boardwalk leading to his hootch. Around him others were running. One man had his flight helmet in one hand and his pistol in the other. His jungle shirt was not buttoned and his boots were not laced. He was heading for the revetments to begin the preflight.

Anderson walked into his hootch. In the light of day, he could see the damage done by the mortar attack. Shrapnel had ripped through the plywood and screen walls of his room. The naked light bulb was broken. The paperback novel he had been reading had a hole through it. There were more holes in his wall locker, and a couple of his uniforms had been damaged.

His flight helmet, stuck down in the bottom of the locker, had not been hit. He grabbed it and then his pistol hanging in the Old West-style holster, complete with ammunition stuck in the loops on the back.

He turned and sat down on the cot. Glancing to the right, he saw that shrapnel had ripped into his pillow. Two pieces of it had penetrated the center of it right where his head would have been if he hadn't moved.

"Damn," he said. He glanced around, looking for someone to tell—someone who would understand what he was feeling. Shrapnel had ripped up his room, and had he not rolled under the cot and then run for the bunker, it would have ripped him up.

He stood, buckled on his gun, pulled his helmet from its bag, and headed out the door. Peter Clarke was coming out of the hootch on the other side of the walk. He was extremely tall, about six-seven, and probably didn't weigh more than a hundred and fifty pounds.

"Hey, Clarke," Anderson said, the awe still in his voice, "you should see my room."

"Why?"

"Shrapnel. I been in there and I'd be full of holes."

Clarke shrugged. "So what?"

"Jesus, what the hell is it this morning? Everybody's running around saying so what."

"I think it means that no one gives a shit," Clarke said.

They walked around the corner of the hootch and across the open field between the officers' hootches and those of the enlisted troops. They stepped up on the boardwalk again and headed toward the operations bunker. It was a heavily sandbagged structure with radio antennas sprouting from the top of it. There was a thick wall of sandbags, four deep, around the outside of it, and a door that opened on a stairway that led down, into the ground. Even that had an appearance of strength. Two-by-twelve-inch planks lined the narrow stairway. At the bottom of it was a rough, wooden door that was closed.

Anderson stood aside and let Clarke walk down the stairway first. Anderson followed closely. As Clarke opened the door, Anderson felt the cool air from the interior. Because of the radio equipment, the operations bunker was air-conditioned. It, the CO's office and hootch, and one of the supply shacks were the only buildings in the company area that were air-conditioned.

Stepping inside, Anderson realized just how hot and muggy it was outside. The sweat began to dry quickly, and he wished that he could stay in the bunker the rest of the day. Or better, the rest of his tour. Even if it hadn't been air-conditioned, he would have liked to stay in it. Shrapnel from both rockets and mortars couldn't penetrate it.

Fox was standing next to a sandbagged wall that had a square of plywood hung on it. Attached to it and covered by a huge sheet of acetate was a map of their operational area. The VC and NVA units were labeled in red and completely surrounded the base camp. No one seemed concerned about that.

Fox sat on a work table, a metal and gray thing that had

probably seen service in Korea. To his right, the bunker opened up into a work room and office for the operations officer. There was a small bookcase holding two dozen black binders, a field phone sitting on his desk, and a couple of aeronautical charts on the wall hidden back there.

There was another room, around a corner, but Anderson had never been back there. It belonged to the operations NCO, and he didn't like anyone bothering him except for the CO and the operations officer.

Fox watched Clarke and Anderson walk in, glanced to the right where the scheduling board was located, and said, "Now that everyone has finally arrived, we can get started."

"Sorry," said Clarke. "Mister Anderson was showing me the damage done to his hootch during the mortars."

"Bad?" asked Fox.

Anderson shot Clarke a dirty look and shook his head. "No, sir. Supply officer will have to get me a new poncho liner and a couple of fatigue shirts." Fox took a deep breath and said, "First things first. Lieutenant Cochran will be evacked to Japan sometime this afternoon. His wounds are serious but not life-threatening. Doc, and a couple of you guys, did a good job getting him out. Mister Crawford took a little shrapnel, but he'll be back in the company area in a week or so."

"Show's that you should use the drainage ditch," said someone.

Fox held up a hand. "We had three others wounded. Supply clerks. They'll be back tomorrow."

"Did Cochran get any flight time in?" asked a lieutenant.

Fox glanced at Captain Aames, who answered, "Got his in-country checkride, CA checkride, and a couple of ash-and-trash missions. Maybe ten, fifteen hours."

"Not even enough time for an Air Medal," commented the lieutenant.

Fox shook his head. "I think we can get him the basic award. The regulation is rather loose, so we can fudge around for that. Aames, you take care of it."

"I'll get with the Awards and Decorations Officer immediately, sir."

"Now," said Fox, shifting gears. "We've got a takeoff scheduled in about thirty minutes. Units of the Twenty-fifth Infantry Division have made contact with a company-sized force of VC and NVA. Our people have taken a few wounded, but they've got Charlie pinned down. We'll be inserting a couple of companies as blocking forces."

"These the people who hit us last night?"

"I doubt that. They're working in the Ho Bo Woods up around the Mushroom." Fox was swinging his feet as he sat on the table. He was gripping the edge and looking down at the plywood as if afraid to look the pilots in the eye.

"This isn't going to be a rough one. LZs are more than a klick from the fighting. We may take a little random fire, but I'm not worried about that."

Clarke leaned close to Anderson. "Christ, we're all going to get shot out of the sky."

"This is an add-on mission," said Fox. "That's why we've had to bump the takeoff times. The scheduled first mission has been canceled, so we'll come back here to Cu Chi to stand by. Any questions?"

Lieutenant Janssen said, "Maps?"

"Right. Operations clerk has prepared a map for C and C and for both flight and gun lead. C and C is airborne now and heading out," said Fox. "If there is nothing else . . ."

Without waiting for the others, Anderson turned and

moved to the counter behind him. The operations clerks were standing there. Anderson glanced up at the scheduling board and saw that he was flying in 693. He set his helmet up on the counter and said, "Need an SOI, and I want a survival radio."

The clerk picked up a grease pencil and wrote the number 14 next to Anderson's name, indicating which SOI he had. Since it contained all the call signs and frequencies of all aviation units and most of the infantry and artillery units, it was a classified document and was controlled.

Anderson stuck the SOI in his pocket. He picked up the survival radio and pulled out the antenna, aiming it at the UHF radio. Flipping the switch to beeper, he heard the receiver begin to wail, telling him the radio was operating. He pushed the antenna down and slipped the radio into his pocket.

The other pilots crowded in behind him. Anderson worked his way through the crowd and opened the door. The heat and humidity rolled over him.

"I think I'll just stay here the rest of the day," he said.

Clarke was behind him again. "Come on," he said. "We've got a war to fight."

# THREE

THE revetments surrounding the aircraft were L-shaped and were made of old sandbags. These were the old cloth bags that had worked well in Europe, but in the tropics they rotted quickly, spilling the sand from them. Maintenance crews were constantly replacing them.

The aircraft were arranged in rows, with the slicks closest to the road and the gunships the farthest away. There were wooden lockboxes near most of the revetments, where the crew chief stored a variety of gear, including the M-60 machine guns.

Anderson walked between two revetments and saw Daniel Nowlin standing near the rotor on a helicopter. He was shaking the inside scissors lever, checking the tolerances there. He crouched and looked down, into the rotor head. Brolin had already mounted the door guns and was standing on the left side of the aircraft with a red rag in his hands.

"Morning, sir," said Brolin.

"How's it look?" asked Anderson, opening the door on the left side of the aircraft.

"Everything's fine."

Anderson put his helmet on the seat, made sure that a chicken plate was there for him, and then moved around so that he could climb into the cargo compartment. He plucked the logbook from the map holder at the end of the console and crouched there checking it out.

"What's this circled red X?" he asked.

"Scratches on the windshield, sir."

Anderson glanced up. The windshield had a few scratches that he could see. It meant that someone had used the windshield wipers without giving the rain time to wash the dirt and dust from the blades. The Plexiglas scratched easily and now, in the rain, the windshield would turn gray, making it difficult, if not impossible, to see through. That was the reason for the warning in the book.

Nowlin climbed from the head and stepped up to the cargo compartment. As Anderson shoved the book back into the map case, Nowlin said, "Everything looks good. What's the deal?"

Anderson jumped out of the cargo compartment and opened the door to the cockpit again. "We've got a couple of early insertions. Missions added on since last night. Let's get this sucker cranked."

Anderson put on the chicken plate, hung his helmet on the hook behind the door, and climbed into the cockpit. He strapped himself in and then began running through the checklist, making sure that everything was turned off.

Nowlin had out a checklist and was running through it, too. Anderson sat back, his hands in his lap, and let Nowlin do the work, watching him. Around them the other aircraft were cranking. The rotating beacons flashed on just before the blades began to turn. The high-pitched whine of the turbines slowly increased until it was a roar wiping out the sound around them.

Nowlin finished, flipped on the battery switch, the start generator, and the start fuel. He rolled the throttle to the flight idle detent and then glanced out the windshield. Turning his head to the right so that he could check the area there, he yelled, "Clear!"

The crew chief yelled back. "Clear!"

As Nowlin pulled the trigger, Anderson grabbed his helmet and put it on. He checked the instruments and then sat back, his foot up on the instrument panel.

When they reached full operating RPM, Anderson turned on the radios and said, "Blackhawk Operations, this is Blackhawk Three Seven. We're up for a commo check."

"Roger, Three Seven. Commo check complete."

"Lead," said Anderson. "You monitor Three Seven is up."

"Roger, Three Seven."

Nowlin came on the intercom. "What's happening here?"

Anderson reached over and switched his control head from Fox Mike to ICS. Using the floor button, he said, "We're going to insert a blocking force. Got a company of grunts in contact."

"The LZ going to be hot?" asked Nowlin.

Anderson shrugged. "I doubt it. Too early in the morning. Charlie shoots at us now and we'll have all day to chase him. Should be cold. Lukewarm at the worst."

"Flight, let's wind them up all the way," said Lead over the radio.

Anderson shifted around, switched the control head back to Fox Mike, and said to Nowlin, "I've got it."

"You've got it," responded Nowlin.

Anderson used the beeper button to run the RPM up to sixty-six hundred. Using the intercom, he announced, "Coming up."

"Clear, sir," said Brolin.

Anderson pulled on the collective slowly but steadily. He kicked at the pedals and felt the helicopter lift up. Hovering three feet above the ground, he said, "Sliding out."

"You're clear sir," reaffirmed Brolin.

Anderson turned the aircraft and saw that Lead was sitting at the edge of the runway. The helicopters were lining up behind him in chock order. Anderson had been listed as Trail, which meant that he was the last aircraft in the flight. He stayed there, watching as the other helicopters maneuvered into position. Once they were all in line, Anderson pushed the cyclic, used the pedals and, hovering to the end of the line said, "Lead, you're ready with ten."

"Roger that." There was a hesitation and then, "Lead's on the go."

One by one, the flight took off. Anderson hesitated, making sure that everyone had gotten off safely, and then pulled pitch, following them.

"Lead, you're off with ten," he reported.

"Lead roger. Come up a staggered trail."

They climbed out to the north, over the runway, the

hangars at the end of it and then the bunker line passing under them. North of Cu Chi was a swampy area and beyond that was the Song Sai Gon.

Lead continued to climb until he reached fifteen hundred feet. He held his airspeed at sixty knots, letting the other aircraft catch him and join on him.

When the flight was formed, Anderson said, "Lead, you're joined with ten in a staggered trail."

"Lead's rolling over."

Following Lead's roll, the flight increased its airspeed to eighty knots and began a gradual turn to the west. It continued on that course, staying south of the Song Sai Gon. Far to the south was a huge swamp that extended toward Cambodia and into the Fourth Tactical Corps area. Highway One, which bordered the northern side of the swamp, was a silver ribbon disappearing into the distance. Just north of it was a fire-support base and, as the flight approached, green smoke began to drift up to it.

"Flight, we'll be landing. Slowing to sixty knots."

Anderson pulled back on the cyclic, lowered the collective, and kicked at the pedals. Glancing at the ground, he could see the infantrymen lined up in a staggered trail formation, six men in each load.

Lead shot approach to the smoke, and each of the helicopters split off to land by one of the loads. Anderson aimed for the last, landed short, and hovered forward. As the skids touched the ground, the grunts moved forward to climb in.

Over the intercom, he heard, "They're all aboard."

Watching the scene in front of him, he waited until the last of the grunts had gotten onto the helicopters. Touching the mike button, he said, "Lead, you're down with ten and loaded."

"Roger. Lead's on the go."

They took off again, and Anderson made the calls telling Lead that everyone had managed to take off and that the flight was joined. The flight flew on, toward the northwest, where the Ho Bo Woods thickened, making it look more like the jungle in the Central Highlands. Across the river was the Michelin rubber plantation with its rubber trees planted in straight rows.

"Lead, this is Blackhawk Five." The executive officer radioed from the C and C helicopter, already on station.

"Go, Five," replied Lead.

"Be advised that you should stay on the northern side of the river until we begin the run in."

"Roger."

The flight turned toward the north, crossed the river, and then headed to the west again. Anderson shot a glance to the south, searching for the point where the grunts were in contact, but he could see nothing of interest.

"Lead, this is Five."

"Go, Five."

"Roger. You'll be landing in about five minutes. We've got arty going in now. You'll be touching down just south of the Mushroom."

"Roger that."

Anderson looked out the front and saw a geyser of silver fountain upward. High-explosive artillery rounds were detonating in flashes of yellow-orange fire. Dirt, water, and debris on the LZ were being thrown up, into the air.

"Lead, we've got last rounds on the way."

"Roger. Turning inbound now."

"Five Six, this is Five."

"Go Five," said Five Six, the leader of the gun team.

"Do you have the flight in sight?"

"Roger that. Turning toward them now."

Anderson saw one of the gunships coming up at the flight. The other two aircraft broke away from him, and raced on along the edge of the flight so that they would be in position to return fire if the enemy was down there.

"I have you in sight, Five Six," said Lead.

The gunship started a steep climb, broke off to the right, and then turned so that it was now out in front of the flight, leading them while diving toward the field where the artillery had landed.

"Last rounds on the ground," announced Five.

"We're inbound," said Five Six.

They began a descent toward the LZ. It was a huge opening in the trees, probably half a klick across. The northern edge was bordered by the river, and there probably would be no enemy soldiers between that and the river.

"Flight, you have full suppression on the left."

The gunship pulled away from the flight, and hovered through the LZ, and two smoke grenades tumbled from the aircraft's rear.

"I have red smoke," said Lead.

"Roger. Land about fifty meters in front of the smoke," said Five Six.

"Roger that."

They were much lower now, closer to the trees where the enemy was supposed to be hiding. Anderson kept his attention on the aircraft in front of him, trying to ignore the possibility that the enemy was close. He didn't want to see the tracers coming up at them because he believed that it would make the tracers hit his aircraft. He knew it was stupid, but he still didn't want to see them.

There was a rapping sound below them and a string of green flashed up. The tracers were pale, washed out in the bright morning sun.

"Flight's taking light fire on the right," Anderson heard one of the other pilots, which one he wasn't sure, report.

"Say ID," said Five Six.

"Roger. Chock Four is taking fire on the right."

Anderson glanced at the trees and saw someone running in the forest. He keyed the mike. "I have somebody in the trees," he said. "This is Trail."

"Roger, Trail."

Behind him the door gun opened fire. He could hear the hammering of the weapon over the sounds of the rotorblades and the roar of the turbine. Red tracers lanced down, struck the ground at the base of the trees, and bounced up, tumbling away.

Now one of the gunships rolled in, firing its rockets. There were twin explosions just inside the trees—puffs of gray-black smoke.

More firing erupted closer to the touchdown point. Two, maybe three AKs on full auto. The rounds, the tracers, flashed past the flight. The door gunners returned the fire. Tongues of flame from the muzzles of the weapons stabbed out. Ruby-colored tracers danced across the ground.

"Flaring," said Lead.

Anderson pulled back on the cyclic and dropped the collective. As the nose came up, there was a series of snaps behind his head.

"Trail's taking hits from the right," he radioed.

"I'm on him, Trail," said one of the gun pilots.

Anderson leveled the skids and touched down. As he did, the grunts leaped from the rear. Two of them fell to the ground and opened fire with their M-16s. The others ran two steps and dived for cover.

"Lead, you're down with ten and unloaded."

"Lead's on the go."

"Taking heavy fire from the right."

As the gunships worked over the tree line, Lead lifted off, dumped his nose, and raced along no more than ten feet from the ground.

The firing from the trees died out. A single stream of green tracers chased Lead for a moment and then stopped. Red tracers, from the door guns and now from the grunts on the ground, poured into the trees.

Anderson shot a glance at the instrument panel. Everything was in the green. He turned slightly and watched as the grunts forced their way into the trees, firing as they moved.

"Lead, you're out with ten. Fire taken on the right," said Anderson.

As the helicopters lifted from the LZ, Captain Brian Morris, a young man who had made the mistake of taking ROTC in college, found himself lying facedown on the ground. He was aware of the hot odor of the dirt, the stink of partially burned JP-4, and the smell of cordite as his men, the door gunners on the choppers, and the VC shot it out.

Morris risked a look and saw the muzzle flashes of an enemy weapon. He popped up, squeezed off a couple of quick rounds, trying to put the slugs into the muzzle flashes, and then dropped again.

"Sir," said Sergeant Shay. He had leaped over a bush and hit the ground near Morris. "We've got to move."

Morris nodded, knowing that the sergeant was right, but he hadn't gotten a good look at the enemy positions. He'd seen one man. He could hear the hammering of a dozen M-16s. There seemed to be no answering fire.

"RTO?" asked Morris, and then spotted the antenna waving in the air twenty or thirty feet away.

"Not much resistance," said Shay.

Morris slipped around, his feet under him, and came up to one knee so that he could see over the tall, dried grass of the LZ. Ruby-colored tracers from his men stabbed into the forest. The gunships were circling overhead but were no longer firing.

"Let's go," snapped Morris. He was on his feet suddenly, running toward the trees. He fired a burst from his hip and watched as the rounds chewed up the ground at the base of the tree line. It had not been well aimed.

As he reached the trees, he was aware that his men had been moving with him. Lead by example, he had been taught. Don't order the attack. Lead it. The men would follow.

He grinned and wiped a hand over his sweat-damp face. He wasn't sure how willing the men would have been if there had been a large force of VC in the trees, but since it was one or two guys, they had moved with him.

Morris pushed his way around one tree. There was a burst from an AK. The rounds slammed into the trunk a foot above his head. Bark rained down. Morris whirled and fired a short burst and then a single shot. There was a shriek, like tires on dry concrete.

"Got him, sir," said Shay.

Firing erupted along the line. An AK stuttered briefly and fell silent. Two M-16s, on full auto, fired, burning through their magazines.

"Fire in the hole," yelled someone.

Morris slipped to one knee and lowered his head. There was the dull explosion of a single grenade. Dirt rained back down, sounding like frying bacon.

"That's got them," said someone..

Morris was up and moving. He found the body of the man he'd shot—a young man dressed in a khaki shirt and black shorts. The shirt was stained with his blood, and his weapon lay near his outstretched fingers.

The captain hesitated there, and then reached out to pat the pockets of the dead man. The intelligence officer had told him time and again to search the dead for documents. The smallest thing could give them an advantage if they were willing to take the time to gather the papers.

Shay appeared at his side. "Resistance has ended."

Morris glanced at the NCO. "Then who's firing?"

"The kids. Burning through their ammo because it's there."

"Stop them."

"Yes, sir."

But before Shay could move the firing tapered off to sporadic shots and then silence. The Americans had secured the LZ and destroyed the enemy force.

"Let's get coordinated," said Morris. "I want a report on any wounded, and then I want the area swept."

"Yes, sir."

Shay turned and moved through the trees carefully, searching for booby traps, spider holes, and enemy soldiers waiting to snipe. Morris shook his head, deciding that it was a stupid way to fight a war. There was no real reason to carry out an assault into the trees. Call in arty or air and let them eliminate the enemy soldiers. Make the war remote control.

He turned and walked back toward the LZ and then spotted the RTO. He snapped his fingers and waved the man over. Reaching for the handset, he said, "I need to contact C and C."

"All set."

He lifted the handset to his ear and thought again, *What a stupid way to fight a war.*

"Flight, give me a damage assessment in chock order," said Lead. He hesitated and added quickly, "We'll be climbing to three thousand feet."

Anderson hit the mike and said, "You've got it."

Nowlin put his hands on the controls and responded, "I've got it."

Anderson used the intercom. "Brolin, you see any damage back there?"

"No, sir. I think the rounds went through the tail boom. No problem there."

Anderson switched back to the Fox Mike. "Lead, you're joined with ten."

"Roger, rolling over."

Anderson listened to the rest of the flight announce the hits they'd taken and then said, "Lead, took some hits in the tail boom. Everything is in the green."

"Roger that. Break. Break. Five did you monitor the status of the flight?"

"Roger that. Wait one." There was a silence and then,

"Lead, take the flight back to the base and have them check the aircraft carefully."

"Roger. What about the second lift?"

"We'll have someone else take care of it. You report to me just as soon as you know the extent of the damage to the flight."

"Roger."

Over the intercom, Nowlin said, "Looks like we'll get out of this one alive."

Anderson glanced at the peter pilot, but didn't say anything to him.

# FOUR

THAT evening the regular officer's call was held in the officers' club. It was the only building large enough to get all the officers into at once. There was a raised stage in one corner, wicker furniture, tables and chairs scattered around the floor, and a bar built into one end. The interior was of plywood that someone had scorched with a blow torch and then varnished to highlight the grain. There were three doors, and huge fans stood near each of the doors, trying to circulate the air because one of the air conditioners was broken.

Anderson, Nowlin, and Nichols sat in the back, close to the bar. Anderson had a Coke, Nowlin had a beer, and Nichols a bourbon and water. There was a small can of barbecued-flavor potato chips sitting on the table in the middle of them.

Major Fox entered, stopped at the bar for a drink, and then walked to the stage. He stepped up onto it and waited until the officers fell silent. He glanced at the roaring fans and the open doors and shook his head.

"I don't want to shout over these things," he said.

One of the officers leaned over and pulled the plug on two of the fans. The club officer shut down the other one and then said, "Two of the air conditioners are working."

"Then shut the doors and turn them on. Might not be cool in here, but it'll be comfortable," said Fox.

He stood there waiting until the doors were closed and the air conditioners working. When he had everything the way he wanted it, he started. "I'll let Captain Stone talk in a moment. First, for those of you who don't know, we had five wounded last night. All will recover. No damage to any of the aircraft, by the way."

"Lousy shots," mumbled a pilot.

There was a ripple of laughter.

"This morning's mission," said Fox, "resulted in the grounding of three aircraft. Maintenance tells me that all three can be airborne tomorrow if we really need them. Right now we're in good shape, though there are a number of aircraft about ready for their periodic inspections. Two weeks from now we might have trouble."

Anderson wasn't interested in that. He was more interested in what the results of the missions had been. Had Charlie been trapped in the field and cut to ribbons? Were there some real results from their flying into the face of death? Or was it just another example of the brass trying to look good without exposing themselves to enemy fire?

Anderson knew that the danger had been minimal—only three or four men firing at the flight as a whole. Not much more dangerous than driving on a highway during rush hour. The difference was that he would be on the highway because he wanted to be. Here, he was flying into the war because those were his orders.

"Ground forces report fourteen VC killed, the recovery of two dozen weapons, both AKs and SKSs, and a single RPD machine gun."

That didn't sound right to Anderson. In the morning they had talked about the grunts having a VC company trapped in the Ho Bo Woods. There should have been more.

Without thinking about it, Anderson was on his feet. He waited until Fox looked at him and then asked, "How'd they get away?"

"Meaning?" asked Fox.

"Meaning, I thought we had an enemy company in there. Most of them got away. And how many of the grunts were killed or wounded?"

"I don't have the casualty figures for our side," said Fox. "I know that there were two medic evac flights before we put in the blocking force."

"Didn't block much, did they?" said Anderson.

"There was too much area to cover," said Fox. "Charlie knows the woods. He knows how to get out."

"That's if he was still there," said Boyle, one of the lieutenants who had gone to the Infantry Officer's Basic Course before flight school.

"Meaning?" asked Fox again.

"Sounds like we ran into the rear guard. Sacrificed themselves so that the main body could get away," said Boyle quickly.

"Okay," said Fox. He rubbed a hand through his short, black hair. "We took a few hits and the whole operation accounted for fourteen dead and some captured weapons. Not a bad haul, all in all.''

Anderson laughed quietly. Except that it had cost a couple of hundred thousand dollars to accomplish that mission, when all the training, equipment, and people involved were counted. It wasn't a very good return on the investment.

Anderson knew that the North Vietnamese were willing to trade lives for eventual success. General Giap had not won at Dien Bien Phu because of his brilliant leadership, but because he hadn't cared how many men were killed in the battle. He had seen his objective, and cost had been no factor. Unfortunately, those directing the American end of the war had not seen their objectives. They were just making the rules up as they went along, with no real goal in mind.

He listened to the rest of the debriefing. Fox called on Stone to go over the day's missions. Anderson didn't care about that because he had been there, watching from Trail. Instead he sipped at his Coke and wondered what was happening at the Gunfighter's Club in Saigon. It had been a couple of weeks since he'd managed to get down there.

When Stone sat down, Fox moved to the center of the stage. He surveyed the officers and then said, ''It's been a while since we let you all make a few comments at one of these things. Anyone have anything to say?''

There was silence for a moment. Anderson knew that everyone was sitting there hoping that no one would stand up with a question or comment. They all probably wanted to have the bar opened so that they could get something to drink and get the hell out of there.

Anderson suddenly found himself on his feet. He said, ''We don't seem to be doing this right.''

"Oh Christ," said Nichols. "Here he goes."

Anderson didn't bother to look at the gunship pilot. He just pressed on. "We concede the night to Charlie. We concede certain areas to him, and we fly home as night approaches. Seems to me that we should be out there with Charlie in the dark, searching for him. We should press him until he has no alternative but to give up." With that, Anderson sat down.

Fox stood there for a moment, rocking back and forth on his heels. He stared at Anderson and then pulled his eyes away. Without commenting on it, he said, "Anyone else have anything he wants to say?"

There was no comment from the floor. Fox nodded and said, "Then we're adjourned."

Anderson stood up and turned. Before he could move, Major Fox was there. Fox asked, "You have a problem, Anderson?"

"No, sir. It just seems to me that if I can see the flaws in our thinking, then the brass hats at the puzzle palace ought to be able to see them. That's all."

Fox nodded as if he was listening and then said, "Let's keep those smart remarks to ourselves. I won't have junior officers questioning orders."

Anderson shot him a glance but said nothing.

"Do I make myself clear?"

"Yes, sir."

As Fox headed toward the bar, Nichols moved in close. "I could have told you to keep your mouth shut. The ring knockers don't want to hear from us citizen soldiers that they are not doing their best. We obey their orders."

Anderson shrugged and then changed the subject. "Is anybody going down to the Gunfighter's Club?"

"Nah," said Nichols. "Too late tonight. Wouldn't have a chance to get into any of the good fights."

"Well, hell," said Anderson. "Hardly any reason to stay awake then."

Nichols raised a hand, almost like a kid in class. When he had Anderson's attention, he said, "On second thought, I have been entrusted with the task of making a test flight on Four Zero One. It's been repaired. Now, I might be persuaded to make that test flight in the direction of Saigon and the Gunfighter's Club."

"I would be willing to buy the first round," said Anderson. "Beer or Coke."

"Not much of an argument," said Nichols. "I'll meet you on the VIP pad in twenty minutes." He turned and walked out of the club.

Anderson crossed the road to the VIP pad as the helicopter was hovering forward. There were rocket pods and miniguns mounted on it, but there were no rockets in the pods or ammo for the guns. Anderson turned his back against the whirlwind stirred by the rotors.

When the aircraft touched down, Anderson, his head down, ran forward and climbed into the back. It was a C-model Huey, which meant there were no wells for the crew chief or door gunner. The bulkhead stretched across the back. There was a single troopseat along it. Anderson sat down on it, buckled himself in, and then held a thumb up when Nichols looked at him.

Sitting in the other pilot's seat was Craig. He was playing with the radios. He paused to glance over his shoulder at Anderson and then turned back to work.

They picked up to a hover, turned, and then began the

climb out to the north. Anderson leaned over and looked down and out of the cargo compartment. It was the first time in a long time that he had been off the camp when he hadn't been flying. It was relaxing to be able just to sit and watch.

The base camp was fairly dark at the edges. In the center there were electric lights and along the runway more lights. But the bunker line was dark. It was a slash of deep black with lighter areas on both sides of it. As they crossed it, Anderson could see the cut-back area of the killing field. In the bright moonlight and starlight, he could see how open it was—how hard it would be for the enemy to cross.

They turned to the east and as they reached three thousand feet, Anderson could see the glow of Saigon. Everywhere in South Vietnam the people feared light. A light at night would draw both the VC and the Americans. Anywhere else a light would draw death to it like a moth, but not in Saigon. Everyone knew where it was and no one feared the light at night.

Anderson shifted around, chilled by the cold air blowing in the cargo compartment. He leaned back against the soundproofing on the bulkhead and closed his eyes. He was feeling depressed and couldn't understand it. He knew that he needed a drink, wanted one, but he could have gotten that at the club. There was no reason to fly down to Saigon.

He opened his eyes and saw that they were approaching Saigon. There was a golden glow from the center of it. Flares hung in the air above the city, floating slowly toward the ground. It underscored the fact that a war was going on.

Craig turned in his seat, pulled the boom mike of his helmet to the side, and yelled, "We'll be landing in about five minutes." He held a thumb up.

Anderson responded by nodding and then wished that he had stayed at Cu Chi. He wasn't in a party mood.

Fox stood at the head of the conference table that was shoved into the far end of his office. His desk was in one corner, a settee stood against one wall, and an air conditioner was built into the opposite wall above a short bookcase.

The conference table was about the size of a kitchen table and had six chairs around it. The executive officer, Captain Stone, the operations officer, and the three platoon leaders were sitting and waiting as Fox paced.

"Gentlemen, I am not happy with this morning's operation and I just had a warrant officer tell me that he wasn't happy with it either."

"Fuck him," said Stone.

Fox shook his head and said, "Under normal circumstances, I would agree with you, but this time I think he was right."

"A warrant officer?" said Stone incredulously.

"A warrant officer," confirmed Fox. "I've been thinking about what he said, and I would like to kick around a couple of ideas. Maybe we can do something to improve the situation."

"There's not much way to improve," said Stone. "We followed procedure."

Fox pulled out the chair and sat down. "Maybe that's the problem. The procedures aren't as good as they could be. Maybe we should look at them and see how they can be improved."

"These procedures," said Stone, "have been working for six months."

"That warrant officer pointed out that we did not go after

the enemy with the enthusiasm we should. We allow Charlie to select the battlefield and the time of the battle. We let him come to us.''

Stone nodded. ''Not much we can do about that.''

Fox sat quietly for a moment and then rocked back in his chair. ''If we examine, carefully, how we structure our missions, maybe we'll see a way to improve them.''

''All this because a warrant officer was pissed off about the way the war is going?''

''No,'' said Fox, ''all this because he was right at the officer's call tonight. The results of the morning's mission weren't all that spectacular when you remember there was a VC company in the trees.''

''So what are we going to do?''

Fox sat quietly for a moment and then said, ''I hope that we'll be able to figure that out ourselves. That's why you're here.''

''For how long?''

''Until we get done,'' said Fox. He glanced at the men with him and knew they weren't happy. To himself, he thought, *Fuck 'em.*

# FIVE

THE road leading to the Gunfighter's Club had giant green feet painted on it. At first there had been only a few of them within fifty feet of the club, but as time went on, the footprints were moved outward so that it was possible to find the club from nearly any point at Tan Son Nhut. Just look for the closest green footprint and then follow it to the next and then the next. Eventually the Gunfighter's Club would loom in the distance. Men who were bored found bizarre ways to amuse themselves.

The club itself was now a two-story building. The front entrance was recessed slightly and had the look of a saloon from the Old West. There was a boardwalk in front of it, and sitting in a chair just outside the doors was a man who looked like a bank guard in Dodge City. His hat was pulled low as if to shade his eyes, though it was now dark, and there was a shotgun across his knees.

"Doesn't look friendly," said Nichols.

"They never look friendly," said Anderson.

As they approached, they heard the driving beat of rock and roll music. Men inside the club were cheering wildly. Anderson stopped short.

"I don't think it's going to be a relaxing atmosphere," he said.

"No," said Nichols, rubbing his hands together like a man who had just been shown the feast after weeks of famine. "Not at all."

The guard sat up and glanced at them. He had to wait for them to move into the light so that he could see if they were all wearing wings. That was the thing about the Gunfighter's Club. Only rated personnel were allowed in. All aircrew members, regardless of position or rank, were allowed access to the club. Anyone who was not rated was not allowed in, regardless of position or rank. The only exception was women. They were allowed in regardless of everything.

As Anderson, Nichols, and Craig approached, the guard looked at their uniforms, saw the wings, and rocked back in his chair. He said nothing to them, but he made no move to stop them either. That was the way he granted permission.

Anderson grabbed the door and opened it to a solid wall of music. Even outside it was nearly deafening. He pushed through the doors and into the entrance that was lined with lockboxes for weapons. No pistols, rifles, knives, grenades, or shotguns were allowed inside.

Anderson pulled at the bottom of his jungle jacket and then lifted it over the pistol belt he wore. By sticking the holster into his front pocket, no one would know that he still had his weapon. Rules and lockboxes notwithstanding, he would keep his weapon. He shot a glance at Nichols, who was now doing the same thing.

They entered the club proper and the noise level rose again. The air was heavy with cigar and cigarette smoke that the slowly turning ceiling fans and the air conditioners did nothing to dissipate.

Opposite the door was a huge bar with four men and two women working behind it. The crowd there was four or five deep, with everyone yelling orders at everyone else. Behind the bar were rows and rows of liquor bottles. Everything that anyone could possibly want to drink was there. And behind that was a huge mirror that was cracked down the middle.

To the left, at the far end of the building, was a raised platform that served as a stage. In a single spotlight was a Vietnamese woman dancing in time to the rock and roll. Her long, black hair was tied back in a ponytail that was whipping around as she danced. She wore a short skirt but no blouse. Her hands were behind her back as she struggled to unhook her bra and keep pace with the music.

In front of her, at the foot of the stage, were a dozen or more GIs waving MPC dollars at her, trying to get her to strip faster. Behind them were tables crowded with more GIs, but sprinkled in among them were flight nurses and women who worked in the embassy or for civilian contractors in Saigon. No one objected to the non-rated women being in the club, with the possible exception of the flight nurses.

Behind the tables were more men standing, watching, and cheering on the dancer. Almost everyone held a drink or a beer and most of them were smoking. They were screaming and yelling. There were members of the air force, some in gray flight suits and some in fatigues, and there were members of the navy, most in gray flight suits. There were army pilots and army crewmen. The club was packed.

Nichols leaned close to Anderson and yelled, "This might not have been the best idea."

"Where else you going to get to see naked girls dancing?" asked Anderson, waving a hand toward the stage. He pushed off into the crowd, searching for a place to stand or sit.

Three men who had been occupying a table stood up, and, before anyone could move in that direction, Anderson had fallen into one of the chairs.

"Hey!" yelled an air force pilot. "We've been waiting all night."

Anderson looked up at him and said, "Who hasn't?"

The air force pilot stood for a moment staring down, but the rules of the club stopped him. Whoever got to the table first got it, regardless.

Nichols shouldered his way through and dropped into one of the other chairs. Craig was slower but finally got there. Just as he sat down, Nichols yelled, "You have to buy the beer."

"I thought Anderson was going to buy the first round."

"True," said Nichols, turning to face Anderson.

He pulled a couple of MPC dollars from his pocket and set them on the table. "We can always wait for a waitress."

Almost as if she had heard the statement, a waitress appeared. She was a short woman with damp, shoulder-length hair, a round face, and a blouse so soaked through with sweat it looked as if it had just been washed.

"You want?" she asked.

"Beer," said Anderson.

"Scotch rocks," said Nichols.

"Coke," said Craig to the waitress and then to Anderson and Nichols: "Someone has to be sober enough to fly."

Anderson turned his attention to the woman on the stage. She had stripped to her bikini panties. Sweat glistened on her body, highlighting her breasts. She had her thumbs stuck into the waistband of her panties and was teasing the audience by flashing them. Finally she danced away from the edge of the stage, turned her back, and shoved the tiny garment to her knees. She danced there for a moment, and, when her panties fell to her ankles, she stepped out of them.

She spun around then, skipped forward, and began to dance. The men cheered her on. She whirled, came up on her toes, and began to caress her own body.

"Better than the movie at the club," said Craig.

The girl stayed on the stage, dancing. The music ended and she stopped, standing there, her chest heaving as she breathed. When the music started again, she hesitated, and then began to dance, first slowly, but then catching the beat.

The waitress arrived and set the drinks on the table. Anderson pushed some money at her, which she grabbed, disappearing into the crowd.

"Guess that was for the drinks and the tip," he said.

"What are you going to do with all that money, anyway?" asked Nichols.

"Well, I could order a stereo system. Or buy a good camera. Or waste it on an R and R. I can find ways to spend it without the help of a Vietnamese waitress," said Anderson. He picked up the beer and took a drink. "At least it's cold."

Craig took a long pull at his Coke and then set it down.

"How come," he asked, "at Cu Chi, there are times when we have to drink warm beer or warm Coke because there's no way to get cold ones? Here in Saigon, they have everything."

"Because," said Anderson, "you've got lots of generals hanging around in Saigon, not to mention politicians. Of course they're going to have cold drinks and anything else they want. Generals get first pick of everything, and if you think we've got it bad at Cu Chi, you should try living at one of the small bases. Hell, at least we've got hot water most the time, hot food when we're there to eat it, and a generator that only breaks down once a week."

"So we shouldn't complain?" yelled Craig, trying to be heard over the cheering and the shouting and the music.

"Hell, it's the way things are," said Anderson. "Be happy that we've got all that we do. It could be a lot worse."

Fox rocked back in his chair and looked at the lined pad on which he'd scribbled his notes. The others around the table looked tired. They looked as if they wanted to get the hell out of there, but Fox wasn't quite finished.

"Stone, you coordinate this with the Twenty-fifth. I want to be ready to go on this tomorrow."

"Sir, it's getting late."

"I know that, but I believe one of the complaints I've heard from our young troops is that the brass treats this as a nine-to-five war. Well, we'll be getting a little overtime tonight."

"Yes, sir."

Fox looked at the platoon leaders. "I want three flight

crews from each platoon. That means five crews flying and one standing down with the spare, if they need it.''

''Rearm?'' said Captain Ford. He was the gun-platoon leader.

''You have a problem?'' asked Fox.

''Well, yes, sir. I think that the guns could be standing by here. I don't have the assets that the others have. What you're asking is that I supply, daily, two heavy gun teams, not to mention Smokey. That's seven flight crews. I can't do it. My men are tired already, and I don't have the aircraft.''

''All right,'' said Fox. ''I want a light gun team standing by here, and by that I mean they'll have to stand by at Dau Tieng or Tay Ninh, and you will be tasked for that.''

''Yes, sir.''

Brown chimed in. ''You're tasking us for the normal of five flight crews and then three additional, plus the ash and trash and the C and C? That's a heavy load.''

Fox leaned back. ''If we fly eight ships in the flight and split the two remaining loads among those eight, we've cut the commitment. You only have to supply a pilot for the C and C, and I think that's good experience, especially for the young lieutenants. Gives them a good seat for how this war is conducted. It's training for them. I'll call Battalion and see if I can get the ash-and-trash requirement lifted. That cuts into the commitment.''

Peters spoke up finally. ''I had the doc down talking to me this afternoon.''

''Christ,'' said Fox. ''Now what?''

''He pointed out that army regulations prohibit more than ninety hours of flight time in a running thirty-day period. The majority of the pilots are over that.''

"But all he has to do is see them to make sure they're in good shape, and we're in the clear."

"Yes, sir, that's right, but about half of them have more than a hundred and twenty hours."

"Meaning?"

"He's supposed to see them on a daily basis or the men are supposed to be grounded until their flight time dips below ninety."

"The way you're going," said Fox, "means that you haven't given me the worst of it yet."

"About ten percent of the pilots have more than a hundred fifty hours. They're all aircraft commanders."

"Shit."

"Yes, sir. And you're proposing that we increase the hours being flown for this mission of yours."

Fox looked from man to man at the conference table and then down at his notes. "When a warrant officer articulates exactly the problems that we face fighting this war, it is time to make a change in that. If the mistakes we make are so blatant that a warrant officer, whose sole mission is to fly airplanes and helicopters, can see the mistakes, then it is obvious that the enemy is going to see those mistakes and exploit them. We had a good example of that this morning. Hell, we had two good examples of it."

"Yes, sir," said Stone. "But does that mean we've got to take on this burden? Especially since no one has ordered us to do it?"

"That your concept of how to fight a war? Do what you're asked to and no more?"

"No, sir. But I wonder about the wisdom of a plan that will overtask our assets without the authority of a higher headquarters. They're counting on our people being here and ready to go when they call for them.''

"I don't see this as a problem," said Fox. "It's an experiment with a limited run.''

"You said nothing about limiting the operation," countered Stone.

"That was implied in the plan. If we run this for two, three weeks without significant results, then obviously we will cancel it. But if it works, we duplicate our staff work, our records, everything, and forward it all up to Battalion as a plan of action.''

"Yes, sir," said Stone. "Still, we're putting a strain on all our facilities. Maybe we should coordinate with the Crusaders at Tay Ninh.''

"Why share the glory?" said Fox. "This is our operation. Nobody said that the tour in Vietnam was going to be easy. We'll just have to put some of the other, less-important projects on hold. Anything else?''

"How do we determine who goes?" asked Brown.

"Volunteers," said Fox, grinning. "Except for Mister Anderson. I think he was volunteering this evening when he made his comments.''

"Getting rid of the rotten apple?" asked Stone, smiling slyly.

"Nope. Putting a man into the position of having to back up what he was saying. He doesn't like the way the war was being run, well, here's a chance to run it a different way. Or rather participate in its running a different way." Fox pushed his notepad away. "That got it?''

"When do you want the list of names?''

"Tomorrow at breakfast at the very latest. Orders to be

cut in the morning, certainly by noon, and the first ships out by 1500.''

"That's cutting it a little fine," said Stone.

"Look," said Fox, "we have no real timetable here. We're setting it up. I'd like things in place tomorrow for implementation the following day, but if that doesn't happen, it's no big deal. But I want it done as quickly as possible. Understood?"

"Yes, sir."

"Then let's get at it. We've got a lot to do if we want to make the timetable." He stood up and opened the office door. As the men filed out, he said, "Tomorrow."

# SIX

ANDERSON had finished his second beer, which he
had bought because Nichols browbeat him into spring-
ing for the second round. The naked girl had finally
danced off the stage and disappeared into the back, but she
was quickly replaced by another woman. This one was fully
clothed, but as the music started she took off everything as
fast as she could.

"Now that's the way to strip," yelled Craig, nodding his
approval.

Anderson glanced at the woman and decided that he no
longer cared how many women were up there taking off
their clothes. He tried to figure it out. If a woman stripped,
left the stage, and then came back, it was like she had
never stripped before. The men who had seen her dancing
there naked thirty minutes before were now screaming for

her to take off her clothes again. It didn't make much sense.

Nichols leaned across the table and said, "Another drink or two, and we'll have to head back."

"The helicopter flyable?" asked Anderson.

"A test flight is just a flight to make sure that everything is working right. All the instruments were in the green, all the controls were working, and the avionics were fine. Test flight is complete. We can sign it off."

"Then there's no hurry," said Anderson.

"Nope."

Anderson turned around and studied the stage. The girl was taller than average, and her hair was lighter than average. She looked as if she had some French blood in her, and when she had taken off her bra, there had been a loud cheer. The Vietnamese had small breasts, but this woman had big ones with large nipples.

"Animals," said Anderson.

"Children," said Nichols. "They don't know how to act in polite company."

Craig was standing up, waving his hand, trying to get the woman's attention. She danced to the edge of the stage closest to them and winked at Craig.

He dropped into his chair and said, "She likes me. Give me a buck."

"Use your own money," said Nichols.

"I didn't bring any. Loan me a buck."

Anderson dug out a wad of MPC and peeled off a dollar. "What the hell?" he said.

Craig was back on his feet, waving the money at the dancer. She saw him, smiled, but stayed where she was, collecting the dollars the air force pilots down front were waving at her.

"We're going to have to head back soon," said Nichols.

"Young Craig isn't going to be happy," said Anderson. "I think he's in love."

"Hell, he's in lust. There's a big difference."

"I hope he knows the difference," said Anderson. He picked up his beer and finished it.

A shadow appeared to his right, and he turned to see a tall, blond woman standing there. Her hair hung to the center of her back, and her bangs brushed her eyes. She had a long, slender face, a slightly pointed chin, and dark eyes. She smiled at Anderson and said, "Hello."

Anderson was on his feet immediately. "Hello yourself. How have you been?"

She looked at the table, but there was no chair for her. Anderson waved her into the one he had just vacated. "Thank you," she said.

Anderson pulled another couple of dollars from his pocket and shoved them at Craig. "Go be a hero," he said.

Craig looked at the money and then nodded. "Be back in a couple of minutes."

The instant he was up, Anderson grabbed his chair and pulled it around, sitting down close to her.

"Who's your friend?" asked Nichols.

Anderson shook his head. "Oh, no. It's not going to be that easy. You watch yourself."

"Don't be an ass," said Nichols.

Anderson stared at him for a moment and then said, "Tom, this is Sandy. Sandy, this is Tom."

Nichols held out a hand and said, "Nice to meet you."

"He looks young too. He another pilot?"

Anderson nodded. "We're not going to have that discussion again, are we?"

"What discussion?" asked Nichols.

"Sandy thinks we're too young to be pilots."

"Well," said Nichols, "so do I. I wouldn't trust me with an expensive aircraft. In fact, I think I should be back home, at school, chasing cheerleaders."

"High school?" asked Sandy.

"College, actually," said Nichols. "I've already graduated from high school."

"We all have," said Anderson. "It's one of the requirements for flight school, though I'm not convinced they stick to it."

Craig returned, looked at the filled chairs, and then stood there. "Somebody give me a buck."

"The romance over?" asked Nichols.

"Not yet," he said. When he got the money, he took off again, pushing his way through the crowd.

Sandy turned her attention to Anderson. "Haven't seen you down here recently."

"The war, you know," he said, grinning. "Actually, we've been flying quite a bit and haven't had the chance to get down here."

"You going to be down here for a while?"

Anderson shot a glance at Nichols but knew the answer to the question. They'd have to be heading back to Cu Chi sometime in the near future. Their major problem would be to convince Craig that the dancer didn't love him. She was only after the dollar bills he was waving at her.

To Sandy he said, "We've got to get going."

She reached out and touched his hand. "You sure you can't stay for a while?"

Anderson leaned forward and said, "I couldn't hear you. That music is so damned loud."

She laughed and let go of his hand. "Forget it. It was nothing."

The dancer that Craig had fallen for exited the stage, and a new girl appeared. She wasn't Vietnamese. She was tall, thin, had blond hair and blue eyes, and looked as if she had been in the United States within the last few weeks.

"Who in the hell is that?" asked Nichols.

Sandy turned her attention to him. "You boys should really get out more. That's part of the new feature here. Anyone can dance. The club pays twenty-five dollars for an hour show, if you strip all the way. If you don't, it's ten bucks."

"Jesus," said Nichols, "I've got to get out more. Do they get anyone to take them up?"

Sandy pointed at the stage. "There's your proof."

"She going to take it all off?" asked Nichols.

"I wouldn't be surprised. A couple of girls were dancing but didn't want to take off their bras or panties, but the audience got so rowdy that they stripped."

"Jesus," said Nichols. "Have you done it?"

Sandy shook her head. "I have a little dignity." Then she grinned. "Besides, there are so few round eyes here that we don't have to strip to get men interested. I think some of the girls do it because no one at home will ever know they did, and it's kind of a kick."

"How would you know?" asked Anderson.

She glanced at him and then at the table. "I signed up to dance one night. I didn't do it. Chickened out at the last minute, but I though about it. Just thinking about it was enough for me."

"I hate to ruin the course of true love," said Nichols, "but we'd better be going."

"I thought you said that it was true lust."

"I wasn't talking about Craig," said Nichols.

Anderson, sitting in the cargo compartment of the helicopter, couldn't help thinking about what might have been. Sandy had been sitting close to him. He had been able to see the swell of her breast inside the fatigue jacket she had worn, and that had been more erotic than the naked woman dancing on the stage. He had felt her warm fingers on his wrist, and that had been more exciting than seeing the sweat glistening on the body of the dancer. Sandy had been more exciting than any of the women in the club, and if he'd had another way to get back to Cu Chi, if he'd known what the schedule for the following day was going to be, he might have been able to spend the night with her.

Instead he had slipped away, moving toward the outside of the Gunfighter's Club while she stayed behind with ten thousand other GIs. Fate had conspired against him. It was worse than living at home during his last year of high school. Then there had always been someone around to ruin the best of his plans.

Leaning back against the soundproofing, insulated from the others by the roar of the turbine, the pop of the blades, and the darkness of the night, Anderson could concentrate on his thoughts. He could think of Sarah, who had told him that she loved him, who had wanted to prove it but hadn't wanted to do it in the backseat of a car or in a motel room. The clerks would had to have known, because there would have been no other reason for two kids who were so young to be checking into a motel.

They'd tried to arrange something for her house or his, but someone was always showing up unexpectedly or not following the script as they had laid it out. Now, tonight, he'd gotten the impression that Sandy was interested in him. She had a room, or there were rooms downtown available from clerks who didn't care, and no one would be questioning them, but he'd had to go home. Dad was waiting up.

"Damn," he said. He could imagine what would have happened. It would have been a night to remember.

He turned his head and looked out into the blackness of South Vietnam and thought it odd that the whole United States Army would conspire to keep him from getting laid. He couldn't be the only helicopter pilot in the whole country. There was no reason for him to have to return to Cu Chi that night. Nothing important was going to happen.

For a moment, just a single moment, he thought of telling Nichols to take him back to Hotel Three. From there he could get to the Gunfighter's Club easily, and the next day he could get a ride to Cu Chi easily. No one would miss him and his friends would cover for him. He'd seen the new lieutenants cover for one another when one had had too much to drink and couldn't get up to go fly. No one cared who filled the slots so long as they were filled.

And then he remembered the difference. The lieutenants had been peter pilots. He was an aircraft commander and, even though a pilot was an aircraft commander for the majority of his tour, it seemed that the army was always short of them. There were never enough of them. He'd have to return to Cu Chi.

Anderson laughed. That was the thing. In high school all the boys had tried to think of ways to get the girls to drop their pants. It had been a big game to everyone. Here, in the adult world, a world that Anderson at nineteen had yet to fully understand, it wasn't the same game. The women could admit that they liked it as much as the men. No cute games about it. Now it was when. And when always seemed to be in the future.

Craig turned in his seat and yelled, "We'll be landing in a few minutes."

Anderson nodded and held up a thumb. He hoped that Sandy would wait a day or two. His priority now was to get a night in Saigon. Once he did, he would find Sandy and things would improve greatly.

Through the windshield, he could see the lights of Cu Chi. The helicopter was crossing the perimeter wire. As it did, Craig turned and waved him forward.

"What?" he asked, crouching right behind the armored seat, a knee on the metal deck.

Craig yelled in his ear. "Operations asked if you were on board. Seems that your platoon leader has a case of the ass because you bugged out without telling anyone."

"Shit. Who cares at night? Nothing going on."

"Right," yelled Craig. "Anyway, as soon as we're on the ground, you're to report to him. He'll be waiting in operations now that you've been found."

"How'd they sound?" asked Anderson.

"Hell, we talked to the clerk. They don't give a shit. They just sit in that bunker, in the air-conditioning, and mark the days off their short-timer's calendar."

"Guess I'll find out when we get there."

"Guess you will."

Anderson moved back and sat down on the troopseat. Wasn't that just the way. Times were mellowing out, the tour in Vietnam wasn't all that bad, and then someone decided it was time to take a crap on you.

"Fuck it," he said, because he could think of nothing else to say.

# SEVEN

**N**ICHOLS landed at the VIP pad and let Anderson out. Anderson, ducking low to avoid the whirling rotorblades, hurried to the edge of the pad and crouched as Nichols picked up to a three-foot hover. Closing his eyes and holding onto his hat, Anderson waited for the dust storm created by the helicopter to subside, and then walked across the road to the operations bunker.

He entered it and walked down the steps until he reached the wooden door at the bottom. There he hesitated, wondering how mad Brown could be. It wasn't as if he had left the platoon shorthanded or had ducked out on a detail of some kind. All he had done, officially, was fly with Nichols on a test flight of one of the helicopters.

He opened the door and was surprised by the subdued lighting in the bunker. Whenever he'd been in it before, the lights had been bright. The scheduling board was wrapped in shadows, and there was no one behind the counter. From the left, where the radios were tucked out of the way, came the pop and buzz of static.

Anderson turned and walked around the corner. Brown was sitting with Peters, a map spread out in front of them. Approaching, Anderson said, "Captain Brown?"

"Where the hell have you been?" asked Brown without looking up.

"With Nichols, test-flying one of the gunships."

"Why would you be doing that?"

Anderson shrugged. "Why not?"

Brown straightened up and turned to face him. He stared at Anderson for fifteen seconds and then said, "You are a wiseass, aren't you?"

Again Anderson shrugged.

"You ever heard the word *sir*? It is used by a subordinate when addressing a superior."

"Yes, sir. I was aware of the custom."

Brown shook his head. Finally he said, "Next time you feel the urge to leave the company area for an extended period of time, you let someone know where you're going, preferably me. That's SOP."

"Sir," said Anderson, "we do not report to anyone or sign out to trot up the road to the PX or to Battalion or anything else. We just hotfoot it down there when the urge strikes. We were off duty."

"In Vietnam you're never off duty," said Brown.

Anderson could see that the conversation was going nowhere. He nodded and said, "Yes, sir."

"Now, we wouldn't have detected your little escapade had you not been shooting your mouth off in the club."

Anderson suddenly understood what this was about. Fox had not appreciated a lowly warrant officer with no college suggesting that the brass didn't have a clue about what they were doing. He'd spoken to Brown, and now the shit was about to roll down on Anderson.

"Yes, sir."

"Now," said Brown, "we're putting together a special mission involving five slicks, two gunships, and thirty grunts—a special mission to eliminate the problems you've mentioned recently."

"Yes, sir?"

"And we're looking for volunteers," said Brown.

"Volunteers?" said Anderson.

Brown dropped his pencil to the desk. "I thought this was something you'd jump at. A chance to go out to face Charlie on his home turf. Show us all that you were right. All we have to do is take the war to Charlie. I believe those, or something close to them, were your words."

Anderson didn't say anything for a moment. He knew that he was being baited. Brown wanted him to volunteer for the job, which meant that he would be gone for a while. Anderson had learned one thing in the army. Never volunteer. It was the way that heroes were made, but it was also the quickest way to get killed. He stood there and stared back at Brown.

"You don't want to prove that you were right and the rest of us were wrong?"

"No, sir," said Anderson.

"Well then, I have some bad news for you, because you have volunteered. Major Fox mentioned it earlier. Thank you and congratulations. Hope you have a good time. You are now dismissed."

"Yes, sir," said Anderson. He turned and headed up the stairs. Outside, in the heat and humidity of the night, he realized that there was another rule that no one had bothered to teach him. Never criticize the brass where they could hear you do it. Talk about them late at night, among the other warrant officers, but never do it in the club after an officer's call, where the brass congregated.

He headed back toward the officer's area and saw Major Fox coming at him. Anderson raised his hand to salute. Fox returned it and then stopped.

"Captain Brown tell you about the meeting tomorrow at eight in the club?"

"No, sir."

"Oh. Have you volunteered for our special mission?"

"Yes, sir, I have. Just now."

"Splendid. I knew you'd feel it necessary once you'd heard about it. See you tomorrow."

"Yes, sir."

The sergeant found Morris sitting on his cot, his radio sitting on an ammo-crate table, tuned to AFVN. His flashlight, also sitting there, created a dim glow as he leaned forward trying to read the latest letter from his wife. She had used a pencil, and he was having trouble making out some of the words.

"Major wants to see you, sir," said the sergeant.

Morris reached over and snapped off the radio. He left the flashlight on, figuring that the army had enough batteries and that he didn't want to trip over anything on his return. There were creatures that wouldn't venture out into the light, and he intended for them to remain in hiding.

He stood up and ducked through the low-hanging entrance. Outside, the sky was lit with the eerie greenish-yellow light of flares. Shadows were swinging in time to the motion of the flares under their chutes. If he had been drinking, or taking drugs, the landscape would look just the way it did now. There was no reason to take drugs when the army went to so much trouble to create a surreal world in which to live.

He found the major in the command post that was built into one section of the commo bunker. It was the strongest structure in the camp, designed to withstand mortars and rockets in an all-out assault. The commo bunker had to survive so that they would be able to get help if Charlie decided that the camp had to be overrun.

Morris entered the bunker, stepped down the three narrow steps, and turned to the right where the major sat. He was hunched over a field desk that didn't look sturdy enough to withstand a strong breeze.

"You wanted me, sir?"

"Ah, Morris. Listen, I got a call from one of the aviation companies, down through Brigade and Battalion, tasking us with supplying sixty soldiers for some kind of special project they've got going. Thought you might like a crack at it."

"Yes, sir. They tell you what it's all about?"

The major shrugged. "They have some wild-ass scheme to put men and aircraft into the air to search for the enemy. No walking around. An airborne search—and when they find something, to swoop in on it like eagles, destroy it, and then get the hell out. Just enough soldiers to insure they won't get wiped out. Quick. Mobile."

Morris laughed. "Sounds like the old cavalry concept adapted to aviation."

"Right. Five ships with half the force, airborne at all times. They see something, and if they need help they call for the second lift." He was speaking rapidly, in a stutter that sounded like machine-gun fire.

"Yes, sir," said Morris.

"The thing that bothers me most about this," said the major, "is that we didn't think of it ourselves. It makes perfect sense, now that someone has thought of it. One of our problems has been getting people into the field when Charlie's been spotted. This way the men are there."

"Seems to me that it would be a real good way to get ambushed by a company of VC. Let these guys spot a patrol and have the patrol lead them into the ambush."

"Except that our side has gunships with the choppers, and they'll be able to call in artillery and air strikes. Sixty guys is not a small force."

"Thirty," corrected Morris. "You don't get to sixty until the second lift gets in."

"Thirty," agreed the major. "I like this idea. Take the war to Charlie like we haven't before."

"Yes, sir." Morris was quiet for a moment. He felt the letter from his wife in his pocket and knew what she would say about it. Don't do it. It's a stupid idea. Except that Morris could see that it wasn't stupid. It made good sense and it brought into play all the advantages the Americans held over the enemy.

"You'll volunteer for this?" asked the major.

"Oh, hell," said Morris. "Why not?"

"I can't promise anything," said the major, "but I think there might be a medal or two in this. Good for career growth, if you know what I mean."

"Yes, sir."

* * *

Nichols found Anderson in the club drinking a beer. The jukebox was turned low, and there were two nurses from the Twelfth Evac Hospital talking to a couple of the pilots at a corner table.

Nichols pointed at them. "Not quite the Gunfighter's Club, but what the hell?" He turned on the stool so that he could lean back on the bar and study the two women.

"Nurses don't come here often," said Anderson, "because most of them want to latch onto a doctor and not a teenage warrant officer helicopter pilot who'll probably be dead in a couple of weeks."

"Now what in the hell . . . Uh-oh. What'd Brown want?"

"Apparently I said too much earlier. They now have a new idea, one that calls for volunteers, and I have been volunteered for it."

"Doing what?"

Anderson grinned. "Now that is the question. I don't know, but I'll find out tomorrow." He glanced at Nichols, who was still watching the nurses. "I understand that they'll need gunship drivers. You could volunteer."

"And I could become an instant millionaire, but I sincerely doubt it."

"It was a thought."

One of the nurses stood up and moved toward the bar. She was wearing a short skirt and light blouse and had short dark hair. She glanced at Anderson and Nichols but apparently didn't see them. She moved to the end of the bar, ordered something, waited for it, and then took it back to the table.

Nichols said, "Now what do those two have that we don't?"

"A college education? A commission? A chance of surviving the next few weeks?"

"You think this thing is going to be that bad?"

"When was the last time they asked for volunteers to spend a couple of weeks in Saigon?"

"A good point," said Nichols. "But they're not going to throw away trained aviators and perfectly good equipment on some wild-ass scheme."

Anderson grinned and said, "I can refute that statement with three words—George Armstrong Custer."

Nichols laughed. "He's not considered the best of commanders by the powers that be. I doubt that Fox wants to emulate Custer. It is not a good career move."

One of the men with the nurses walked over to the jukebox, fed it, and began pushing buttons. The music changed a moment later, and the three others moved into the open area that had been optimistically labeled a dance floor.

"The show is beginning," said Nichols.

Anderson nodded and then said, "If you hadn't had to get back so badly, I might have arranged something."

"If I hadn't been in such a hurry," Nichols responded, "you might have found yourself volunteering to be Custer's chief scout. Hell, I did you a favor."

Anderson turned away from the dance floor and looked at the bartender. He was one of the lieutenants whose additional duty was club officer. He stood there, arms folded, watching the two women dance.

The men dancing with them were having a good time teasing everyone else. They spun the women, causing their skirts to swirl, showing off the colored panties they wore. Anderson wondered if the nurses knew what was happening, and then decided they had to. It was all part of the plot to ruin his day and his life. The entire army was against him for some reason. He couldn't figure it out but knew that it was true. The army was going to destroy him.

"I guess I'd better go get some sleep," he said finally. "Tomorrow I find out what I volunteered for."

"Look at the bright side," said Nichols. "They can't kill you. Well, they can't eat you, anyway."

"Thanks. I appreciate that."

Nichols nodded. "Anytime."

# EIGHT

"**I**T'S called Operation Eagle Eye," said Major Fox, standing on the stage and looking out at the men who had volunteered for it. "The concept is simple. We put people in the air with one task. Find the enemy. When we do, we land to engage them. We hit them and then we get the hell out. It's what air mobility is all about."

Anderson sat in the dark, at the rear of the group of aircraft commanders and peter pilots. Crew chiefs and door gunners were not invited. Anderson also noticed that there were no representatives from the gun platoon, and that bothered him greatly.

Fox stood for a moment and then said, "There isn't much difference between this mission and those we normally fly. Rather than having a target selected when you take off, however, you'll be searching for a target. If none is found, then you won't be landing. If someone stumbles into contact, then you might be called on for reinforcement. What we have is a quick-reaction team, airborne most of the time, or on standby.''

"But just five ships and what, thirty, thirty-five grunts?'' asked a pilot.

"Precisely. During the daylight hours, Charlie is rarely seen in force. With guns and air support available, the force should be large enough.''

"Where are we going to stand by?'' asked Anderson.

Fox turned to the easel that was beside him and removed the cover sheet. He pointed at a spot in the middle of the Ho Bo Woods. "There is a small ARVN outpost there. We'll move a couple of fuel trucks in, though the POL facilities at Dau Tieng and here aren't that far away. Both of them can be used during the day.''

"Jesus,'' said Anderson.

"You have a problem, Mister Anderson?'' asked Fox.

"No, sir. I'm just not thrilled with having that many armed Vietnamese around us.''

"That's understandable,'' said Fox.

The rear door opened and four pilots from the gun platoon entered. Anderson turned and saw that both Nichols and Craig were there. He held up a hand. Nichols came toward him and sat down next to him.

On the stage, Fox was saying, "Now that the guns have arrived we can get down to specifics.''

Anderson leaned over and whispered, "What the hell are you doing here?''

"Ford told us they needed a couple of volunteers for a special mission, and I remembered what you had said last night. I figured I would be able save your butt.''

"Thanks.''

Fox pulled the map off the easel and set it on the floor. He explained the table of organization, that Lieutenant Elway would be in tactical command with Lieutenant Gates as his second. If it went beyond that, it would be the senior aircraft commander. He looked at Anderson and then continued. He told them about the radio contact schedule. He talked about maintenance problems, that the fuel trucks and the special equipment would be leaving in an hour. If they found the need for anything else, well, they had radios and helicopters and all they had to do was ask for it. He'd do what he could to get it for them.

"Who's going to be gun lead?" asked Fox.

Nichols raised his hand.

"You coordinated with Captain Ford?"

"Yes, sir. We'll be monitoring the radio in case we're needed by the company."

Fox nodded, was quiet for a moment, and then said, "I'm going to get a couple of EMs assigned for a constant radio watch. We'll have them join you in a day or so at the camp. Are there any questions?"

"How long are we going to be doing this?" asked Anderson.

"Three weeks. We want to see how well it works. If it seems to be going well, we'll rotate the crews."

Anderson nodded. He decided that he wouldn't mind being out of sight of the brass for a couple of weeks. Maybe they would do something worthwhile. Maybe they would accomplish something more important than boring holes in the sky. And maybe it would keep him out of trouble.

"One other thing," said Fox. "Each of you will draw an M-16 and two hundred rounds of ammo. At the camp, you won't have access to weapons, and there is always the possibility that you'll need them."

"Great!" said one of the pilots.

"Check in operations," said Fox. "Aircraft assignments have been posted. Lieutenant Elway, please wait behind. If there are no other questions, the rest of you are dismissed until noon, when you'll start preflights."

Anderson pushed back his chair and stood up. "Now tell me again the real reason why you volunteered for this?" he asked Nichols.

"Someone has to keep you out of trouble."

"I thought that's what you said."

Anderson strolled out to the flight line after lunch and found Nowlin crawling over his aircraft. Anderson hadn't bothered to notice the name of the peter pilot assigned to him, but was glad it was Nowlin. Although a new guy, he had a flare for flying. He wasn't like some of the new guys, who had a hard time finding the aircraft, let alone flying it.

"You see anything wrong?" asked Anderson, standing on the ground, his hands on his hips.

Nowlin, who was up on the top checking the rotor head, sat down, his feet dangling over the cargo compartment. "Nope. Seems okay. Book checks out."

Anderson tossed his helmet into the rear and then unshouldered the M-16 and the bandoliers of ammo he carried, dropping them to the cargo-compartment floor. Stepping back, he asked, "You ready?"

"Gear's stored under the troopseat. M-16 and ammo are on the seat. I'm ready."

"You volunteer?" asked Anderson.

"Sure. Didn't you?"

"Nope. I was sort of volunteered. I think that if I hadn't joyfully suggested that it was fine, they would have made it clear that I was going anyway."

Nowlin turned to the left, pushed, and slid down the curve of the rear of the cabin of the Huey, landing on the ground. "When do we take off?"

"I think the grunts are going to hotfoot it over here, and we all fly out together."

"I didn't hear Fox say anything about checking that camp out. There a place to land all the aircraft? Inside the wire, I mean."

"I don't think that the brass hats would make such an elementary error, but we can always hope. I'm going back to get my shaving kit and other gear."

"I'll wait here."

"Suit yourself," said Anderson. He walked out of the revetment area and across the road. He didn't stop as he passed the Orderly Room, because there was nothing to say to any of the people in there. He could have irritated Fox by asking if anyone had flown over the base, but figured it would cause more trouble if he kept his mouth shut. If the camp didn't have an area for the aircraft, Fox and the boys would have to scramble to get something accomplished.

In his room, he pulled out his duffel bag, stuffed his spare boots in the bottom, shoved a couple of sets of fatigues in on top, pushed a Nomex flight suit in on those, though almost no one wore the Nomex, and added his shaving kit, a couple of paperback books, and then a six-pack of Coke. He closed the duffel bag and then sat down on his cot.

The room wasn't much, just a plywood box that was inside a hootch. His fan at the end of the bed helped keep him cool enough to sleep. The cot wasn't that comfortable, but it was his. There weren't a lot of creatures living in the hootch with them. Someone had told him a snake had been seen once in the company area, but that had been months earlier. There were no rats or mice, though the cockroaches were big enough to masquerade as mice sometimes.

The thing was, he knew the horror of the hootch, of Cu Chi and the Vietnamese around him. He did not know what was going to happen at the camp he was going to. He didn't know a thing about living in a bunker with rats and snakes. He didn't know what he would do to pass the time if they didn't have radios or books or lights. He was not thrilled with the prospect of living in the field with a bunch of Vietnamese who were probably all Vietcong as well.

He glanced at his watch and stood up. He shouldered his duffel bag and began the walk out to the airfield.

He reached the aircraft, stuffed his duffel bag under the troopseat, and then climbed in. He pulled a book out of his pocket and began to read, ignoring the sounds around him. He didn't care about the noise of the other helicopters operating on the airfield. He didn't hear the high-pitched roar as an OV-10 Bronco took off. And he didn't hear the artillery as one of the batteries fired to the north.

Nichols approached, climbed in, and sat down on the rough metal floor. "We're ready to go," he announced.

"So," said Anderson.

"Some thanks," Nichols said. "I volunteer to save your butt and all I get is a so."

"Thanks," said Anderson.

On the road, Anderson saw a truck stop. A half-dozen soldiers jumped from the back. They gathered around it as someone began tossing gear out to them.

"Looks like the grunts have arrived," said Anderson.

Nichols turned and watched for a moment. "I think, if I didn't fly, I'd volunteer to be a clerk."

"They'd never take you."

Nichols grinned slyly. "Sure they would. I know the secret of being a clerk. I can type sixty words a minute. The first sergeant or the admin people find that out and I'd be a clerk. It's the only class in high school that looked as if it would be an advantage."

Anderson laughed out loud. "I think we could sell this idea. With all the turmoil on campus, all the guys trying to avoid the draft to stay out of Vietnam, and the answer is simple. Learn to type and then tell the army."

Nichols nodded. "And the very minute the army learns of this ability, you're a clerk, safe from the goons in the infantry. An army travels on its triplicate forms and not on its stomach, as some people think."

Another truck pulled up behind the first, and then a third and a fourth. An officer wearing a harness, a holster with a .45, and two canteens left the men on the road and crossed into the revetment area.

"He's looking for Elway," said Anderson. "Wants to know what to do with his troops."

"And what should he do?" asked Nichols.

"Split them into loads of six or seven and get them over to the aircraft they'll be using. Let us get the helicopters cranked and out of the revetments, and then board."

"Why don't you go tell him that?"

"Because I'm not a lieutenant. I'm just a warrant officer—a technician and not a tactician."

"Of course," said Nichols.

They watched the infantry officer wander around the revetments, until he finally found a lieutenant to talk to.

Happy with the lieutenant's words, he returned to the trucks and started to get the men organized.

"I don't like the looks of this," said Anderson.

"Meaning what?"

"They're going to put us to work."

At that moment Elway appeared in the doorway of the operations bunker and waved a hand over his head. Anderson saw him and pointed. "Told you."

Nichols leaped out of the cargo compartment but didn't leave. Instead he said, "We've got a couple of cases of beer. We'll get the club set up tonight."

"I've only got a six-pack of Coke."

"Shows that you slick drivers don't think far enough ahead. Coke? Christ."

"Maybe maintenance will need us to test-fly a helicopter," said Anderson. "You can never tell about a thing like that."

Nichols shrugged. "Could be. Well, I guess I'd better hotfoot it over to my aircraft." He stopped and then asked, "How bad could it be?"

"Real," said Anderson. "It could be worse than being sent here, and until that happened the worst thing to happen to me was having a tooth filled. That took a couple of minutes. This is taking a whole year."

"Three weeks," said Nichols. "Just three weeks."

Anderson grinned and couldn't help himself. "God created the whole universe in six days. We've got more time than that for everything to go wrong."

"Well," said Nichols, "at least you're an optimist."

"There is that," said Anderson. He pushed himself up and moved around to open the door to the cockpit. Nichols started off again, toward the gunships. As he did, Anderson wondered once more how he got himself into the messes he did. Talent, he decided. He had a talent.

Morris, having learned that they were in the right place, returned to the trucks. He found Sergeant Shay standing by the door of the lead vehicle.

"What's going on, sir?"

"This is the right place. Get the men divided into five loads. Each man's responsible for his own gear and what squad equipment is assigned to him. Once we get that done, we'll head over to the choppers."

Shay stepped past Morris and yelled, "Give me a line right here."

Morris leaned to the side, against the front of the truck. He glanced up, into the cab, where the driver sat waiting for permission to return to the company area. *Fuck him* thought Morris. He'd be in the club that night eating well while Morris was at some rinky-dink little camp.

"Troops are ready, Captain," reported Shay.

From the airfield came the sound of choppers starting up. Morris straightened and watched as the blades on one helicopter began to swing.

"You ride on a different bird than me, sergeant," said Morris. "Just in case."

"Yes, sir. Lieutenant Davis will be bringing the second group down here in about thirty minutes."

Morris nodded. He knew that Davis would put his men into the vehicles that were being sent out to the camp. They would be security for the convoy.

One of the choppers moved from the revetment, out into the open area. It hovered there for a moment and then maneuvered toward the runway on the other side of the revetment area. A second followed the first, and then a third and fourth, and finally the last one.

As the choppers dropped to the ground, and the dust stirred by them settled, Morris waved a hand above his head. "All right men, let's get moving."

They stepped from the road, crossed the dry ditch at the edge, and climbed up and out. They filtered through the revetments and moved toward the waiting aircraft. Morris walked toward the lead ship and then stopped outside the rotor disk, waiting for a moment.

The hand of one of the pilots appeared and waved them forward. The men ducked and rushed in, toward the cargo compartments, climbing up. Morris waited until everyone was in a chopper and then watched as Shay climbed into the last aircraft in the line.

Satisfied that no one had escaped and no one would be left, Morris moved into the lead ship. He climbed up, around one of his men sitting in the doorway, and sat down on the troopseat. As he buckled the belt, the aircraft lifted up to a hover.

One of the men grinned at him and held up a hand. They didn't mind where they were going because they wouldn't be sleeping in the Ho Bo Woods or in the jungle. Tonight they knew they'd be at a camp, not as comfortable as Cu Chi, but a lot better than being out in the boondocks.

Morris held up a thumb, grinning, and reminded himself that he only had another two months before he picked up a staff job. No more crap in the field. Sixty days to safety. He knew his wife would be pleased.

# NINE

THEY took off to the north and then turned to the west. They were following the path they had used a couple of days before. Anderson held the cyclic loosely in his right hand, and the collective in his left. He watched as the flight formed a staggered trail and made the radio call.

This was the best flying. Two thousand feet, above effective small arms range, and, even through it was the middle of the afternoon, the air was smooth. The only buffeting came from the rotorwash of the aircraft in front of him, and, by increasing his altitude slightly, he was out of that. Nothing for him to worry about.

Glancing out and down, into the Ho Bo Woods, he could see the red dirt of the ground. To the south was the circular path that was a fire-support base. It contained six howitzers, and a couple of infantry companies for protection. The howitzers could fire on enemy forces anywhere around the base for eight or ten miles. Anderson and the flight would be under the protective umbrella of that fire base as well as a number of others.

From the right, close to the river, there rose a sudden string of glowing green. It climbed up but missed the flight by a klick or more.

"Lead, got some fire on the far right."

"Say again."

"This is Trail. We just took some fire from the far right. Close to the river."

"Trail, this is Five Nine. Can you pinpoint that fire for me?"

That was Nichols, Anderson knew. He keyed his mike and said, "Close to the river, back about a klick. There's a thick patch of woods. It came out of there. One weapon on full auto. Looked as if he fired the whole clip at us."

"Roger, Trail. Lead, say intentions."

"Roger, Five Nine. We'll continue on to the camp."

"Roger that."

Anderson saw the gunships for a moment as they turned back toward the river. He figured they wouldn't be able to find the guy, who was probably now out in a rice paddy, up to his knees in his work. It was the perfect cover for them. Fire a few rounds at the Americans, hide the weapon, and then get back to planting rice.

A moment later Anderson saw the camp in front of him. The center of it was an old French fort—a triangular structure built close to the ground. The defenders stood in trenches and either fired over the top of the short stone walls or through ports in the walls. The design made it difficult for attackers to get at it.

The camp had been expanded so that the French fort was the redoubt where the defenders would fight if the outer perimeter was overrun. The outer perimeter was built of sandbagged bunkers and rows of concertina wire and tanglefoot. On the western side was a long, level strip where the helicopters would be parked. It was inside the wire, inside the bunker line, but exposed to anyone attacking from that direction.

As the flight approached, someone ran out of a bunker, stopped, and tossed a smoke grenade onto that strip. The light wind swirled around, and the smoke rose gently, telling the pilots that they could land from any direction.

Lead set up the approach, descended, and crossed the wire with the flight right behind him. They touched down, with Lead putting his nose right on the smoke.

Near the bunker line, there was a single American. He stood there, jerking his index finger across his throat. Anderson knew that he wanted them to shut down, but waited for the order from Lead.

"Flight, let's shut them down."

"Five Nine, say status," said Anderson.

"We have negative movement down here. You sure that you saw something?"

"Roger that."

Lead broke in. "Five Nine, come on over here and join us at the camp."

"Roger."

Anderson rolled the throttle to the flight idle detent and watched the gauges. He let the EGT drop, giving the engine a chance to cool slightly before shutting it down completely.

While running, it sucked air into the inlet filters, but once it was shut down, the airflow halted. That meant that in the first few minutes, the temperature in the turbine could rise.

He flipped on the forced trim and let go of the cyclic. He unbuckled his seat belt and slipped down in the seat so that he was more comfortable. When the temperature in the turbine had dropped enough, he held up a thumb so that Nowlin would cut the engine.

As the turbine and rotorblades slowed, the crew chief came around and opened Anderson's door. Anderson climbed out and stood there, looking at the bunkers, at the low hootches that were little more than plywood and screen squares, and shook his head.

"Home, sweet home."

The grunts climbed out of the helicopters and moved deeper into the camp. They formed a ragged line facing the aircraft. Anderson stepped back and sat down on the edge of the cargo compartment and watched as the officers and NCOs moved among the grunts.

Glancing to the right, he saw Lieutenant Elway standing by his aircraft, waving at them. He turned and said, "Looks like we've got a meeting."

Nowlin nodded and started walking up toward Lead. Anderson joined him and said, "I don't think this is going to be a great deal of fun."

"Neither do I."

It turned out there were fifteen American advisers in the camp. They had built several hootches from material they had flown in. Their hootches were in the center of the camp, protected by the perimeter, the bunkers, and finally the Vietnamese quarters.

The man who had thrown the smoke had walked over to them, introduced himself as Captain George Kerns, and told them that the advisers had tried to have some tents erected to house the new arrivals. He glanced first at the pilots and then turned to look at the grunts, and shook his head.

"Never expected this many people, though." He had waved toward the center of the camp. "If you'll get your gear and follow me, we'll get you all set up."

Anderson had walked back to the helicopter, picked up his M-16 and bandoliers of ammo, and then retrieved his duffel bag. As he walked toward the center of the camp, he decided that he didn't want to be that far from his rifle again. He'd have to relearn the lessons of basic training. Your rifle is your best friend and don't go anywhere without it.

They were led to a small tent city set up on what looked to have been a soccer field. That was the thing about Vietnam. There were soccer fields everywhere, and when landing was impossible in most places, there was a soccer field close by that provided an open, level area.

There were six four-man tents standing in two neat rows. The flaps had been raised for the afternoon breezes that never came. Army cots had been erected in them, four cots to a tent. There were footlockers next to each cot but no locks for them. No one had told Anderson or any of the others to bring locks.

"I want the aircraft commanders here," said Elway. "Pilots there, and crew chiefs and gunners there and there."

"Five men in each tent?" asked Anderson.

"No, four aircraft commanders here. No, that's one lieutenant and three warrant officers."

"And you forgot the gun team."

"They can stay together in two of the tents," said Elway finally.

"How about this," said Anderson. "I'll take that cot there. Now the rest of you can figure it out for yourselves."

Nowlin shook his head. "I think I'll just sleep in the back of the helicopter."

"That's not going to work," said Anderson. "Charlie mortars this place and the first thing he's going to aim at is a helicopter."

"I want everyone together," said Elway.

"Nowlin, take that cot," said Anderson.

Nowlin moved forward and dropped his duffel bag to the wooden floor. He sat down on the cot Anderson had pointed out and said, "I'll take this one."

Elway watched as the men spread out into the tents, finding places for their gear. As they did, Anderson said, "No hassle this way. No one complains."

"We're supposed to be a military organization with me in command."

"A word of advice," said Anderson. "Don't do too much commanding. We know our jobs. Let us do them without a hassle and everything will run smoothly."

"I'm in charge," repeated Elway.

Anderson nodded and then said, "You want something to command, then how about this? As I understand the concept, we're to seek out the enemy, swoop in on him, and destroy him anywhere we find him."

"What's the point?"

"Simply that we took some fire on our way here, but you didn't react to it. We were set. We could have swooped in, but we didn't. Think about that."

"I wasn't thinking," said Elway. "My orders were to get us here and set up."

"That's what the problem has always been," said Anderson. "Everyone has another mission. Charlie pops up but it's inconvenient to attack him."

"Is it too late now?"

Before he could answer, there was the sound of helicopters in the distance. They all turned and watched as the two gunships, flying low, came into view.

"I suppose I'd better walk over there and see if they need anything." Elway stood.

But now Kerns returned, leading another officer behind him. Elway said, "Here comes the infantry."

Kerns stepped up and said, "Do you know Captain Morris?"

Elway said, "I spoke to him briefly. Captain, I'm Lieutenant Elway. These are two of my pilots, Mister Anderson and Mister Nowlin."

"Greetings," said Morris. "Though maybe we should coordinate a few things between us before we put this plan into motion. I don't want to find my butt hanging out with no hope of support."

"We don't intend to strand you," said Anderson. "Rule of the game—never leave an American in trouble."

"What about the Vietnamese?" asked Kerns.

"Fuck 'em," said Anderson.

Elway shot him a nasty look and Kerns said, "Don't let the Vietnamese hear you say that."

"Never," said Anderson.

Morris sat down on one of the footlockers. He folded his hands together, stared at them for a moment, and said, "I have to know what your attitudes are toward this . . . this Eagle Eye business.''

Anderson knew that he was trampling all over military courtesy. He should have let Elway answer first because he was senior, but Anderson didn't want Kerns to get the wrong impression about the pilots.

''I think someone finally thought of something that might put the hurt on Charlie. Handled right, Charlie would be forced to move his operation north, where the jungle would get in his way, or to the south, where there is very little cover. And it would show Charlie that we have a few people who can think beyond DEROS and a return to the World.''

Morris grinned. ''When I volunteered for this, or rather when I was volunteered for it, I could see a giant cluster fuck on the horizon—the worst pilots with bad attitudes thrown into this thing. I selected the soldiers with an eye to those who knew what was happening and might have a chance of surviving. Sounds like you guys had the same thoughts.''

Anderson scratched his head and said, ''Don't get me wrong. We're not a bunch of heroes. Our CO asked for volunteers too, and I think some of the guys are actually volunteers, but you've got good pilots. We know our jobs.''

Morris clapped his hands together. ''Great. Now, how are we going to go about this?''

Elway spoke. ''One of two ways. I can operate one ship as a scout with troops on board while the flight either waits here or orbits around, fully loaded, as we search for the enemy. Or, each ship can search a sector and call for the others if he finds something interesting.''

''I'd say we should all stick together with everybody airborne,'' said Anderson.

"Means we'd be flying for about two hours straight if nothing happened. Toward the end of that time, fuel would become critical."

Morris nodded. "Then we search in hour-and-a-half blocks, refuel and piss, and begin again."

"In the morning," said Elway.

"First thing," agreed Morris.

"Not too early," said Anderson, but knew they wouldn't listen to him. They'd start at first light if they could. The army always started at first light.

"First thing in the morning," said Elway.

# TEN

ANDERSON had pointed out that he was more valuable in Trail. He suggested letting Lieutenant Gates fly in Chock Two. With Lead playing scout, Chock Two became the lead. Although there was no basis in military tradition for the argument, Anderson had won by saying that a commissioned officer would then be in command of the flight, and not a warrant officer. Elway overlooked the fact that Anderson had been flight lead more than once.

Now they were orbiting the Mushroom at fifteen hundred feet. North of the river was the Michelin rubber plantation. They knew that Charlie operated in there, using the closely planted rubber trees for protection, but they also knew that an assault into there could lead to an international incident. The plantation belonged to the French, and any fight that started in there would result in trees being damaged.

They also knew that Charlie operated in the Ho Bo Woods. They could attack him there and not have to worry about rubber trees. Elway, in Lead, was now buzzing around at treetop level, searching for the enemy.

They turned again, and Anderson was suddenly bored with it all. He said, "You've got it."

"I've got it."

When Nowlin put his hands on the controls, Anderson let go. He flipped the NAV radio over to AFVN and listened to the DJ playing the afternoon load of rock and roll. He'd heard that early in the war the station had played nothing but Lawrence Welk and big band music. Now, with the majority of the soldiers still in their teens, the station played rock and roll.

"Chock Two, this is Lead."

There was a moment of confusion as the pilots tried to figure out which Lead was calling which Chock Two, and then Gates, in what was now Lead, said, "Go."

"Bring me the flight."

"Roger that."

Anderson sat up suddenly and touched the floor button on the intercom. "Brolin, let the grunts know that we've got something going on."

"Yes, sir."

"This is Lead. Do you have me in sight?"

Gates responded. "Negative. Wait one, I see you now. Low and to the left."

"Roger that."

Lead made a sudden turn, rolling around, but then his nose came up and he was hovering five hundred feet in the air as the flight turned toward him.

"Join on me," he said.

"Roger."

"Five Nine. Say location."

"I'm behind the flight but on the deck. I have the flight in sight."

"Set up on the left side. You will have suppression on the left."

"Roger that."

They caught up with Lead, who was now flying at fifty or sixty knots. Anderson keyed the mike. "You're joined with all five."

"Rolling over."

They stayed low though, no more than five hundred feet above the ground. Lead came on the radio again. "There is a clear area about a klick to the west. That is our destination."

Anderson was on the intercom again. "Tell these guys that we're going in. Watch it on the left."

"Yes, sir."

"Flight, we have full suppression on the right and left," said Lead.

"Lead, what did you see?"

"Ah, wait one."

Anderson could see this was another area where they would have to talk. If Lead had information about what they could expect on the ground, he had to share it regardless of the security aspects. The odds that Charlie would have a radio and be using it on the right frequency were remote. Besides, they were on their way—Charlie had to be able to hear and see them. Nothing would be given away.

"We think we have three, maybe four VC in the woods. We're going after them."

"Roger," said Anderson. On the intercom he asked, "You get that?"

"Passing it along," said Brolin.

Anderson could sense the change in the back of the helicopter. Up to that moment, the Huey had been out boring holes in the sky, and the threat of action had been something in the future. Now the aircraft was heading in to where the enemy was supposed to be—maybe not many of them, but the enemy, armed, nonetheless. The grunts were suddenly tense, alert, excited.

"Coming up on the LZ," said Lead.

Anderson said, "I've got it."

"You've got it."

"Stay with me on the controls," he said. "Just be there, in case."

Nowlin didn't answer.

"That's our LZ directly in front of us," said Lead.

Anderson glanced to the left but could see no movement. He fell back a little in the formation, watching the other aircraft. Lead's door guns opened fire, the ruby-colored tracers flashing out and down.

"Flaring," said Lead.

The door guns behind him opened fire. There were no targets out there. The theory was that five machine guns firing into the trees would keep Charlie from shooting up at the flight. The gunships rolled in, the lead ship firing a minigun. It sounded like a buzz saw cutting through a thick plank.

As Anderson leveled the skids, he heard firing from the trees. A single AK, maybe two of them. He saw no tracers. He dropped the collective and the helicopter touched the ground. The instant the skids were on the ground, the grunts dived off into the thick grass.

"You're down with five. Fire from the left."

"Lead's on the go."

The grunts, now clear of the aircraft, opened fire too—M-16s on full auto. Tracers flashed into the woods. There was a single explosion at the base of a tree as one man used his M-79 grenade launcher.

The helicopters came up, off the ground, but stayed low. There was a flashing in the trees as someone fired at them. The door guns continued to hammer. Lead broke to the right, away from the enemy soldiers.

"You're out with five. Fire on the right."

Morris crouched behind the armor seat in Lead and held onto the inertia reel at the base of it so that he didn't lose his balance. His M-16 was clutched in his left hand and was set on safe.

He glanced at the men in the cargo compartment with him. Three were on the troopseat, and there was one sitting in the right door and one in the left—six men, armed with M-16s and M-79s. Each had two canteens and a first-aid kit, and one man had a PRC-25. Just enough equipment for an hour or two in the field. Enough ammo, more than enough, for a firefight.

The pilot leaned around and yelled, "Taking a little fire down there."

Morris nodded and yelled at the troops. "Going to be hot. Unass as quickly as possible." He flipped the safety off, thought about it, and put it back on. He kept his thumb against it so that he could flip if off the instant he was on the ground.

He moved around, centering himself in the door so that he could look down on the trees and search for the enemy.

He watched the tracers from the door guns and then the gunships rip into the woods.

When the aircraft flared, Morris was thrown off balance. He lifted a hand, caught himself, and then felt the helicopter touch down. As the skids hit the ground, he leaped from the cargo compartment, took three running steps, and threw himself to the ground.

Around him there was firing—his men using their M-16s, the M-60s mounted on the choppers, and an AK or two. He came up, on one knee, and searched for the enemy.

The helicopters lifted off, taking the roaring of the turbines and the popping of the rotors with them. Slowly, it got quieter in the LZ. He heard a short burst from an AK and turned toward the sound.

Shay was up, waving two men forward, attacking the trees. One man was firing from the hip—short bursts, three or four rounds each, into the forest.

Morris leaped up, waved an arm in the classic infantry follow-me pose, and ran forward. The sound of the choppers had faded, and the gunships had backed off so that Morris and his men could attack.

At the edge of the trees, he stopped and crouched. He scanned the forest but saw no movement. An AK fired suddenly. That was answered by two, three, a half-dozen M-16s.

"Anyone hurt?"

"No, sir."

"Let's move on in slowly."

Morris got up and slipped forward. He stepped around the trunk of a small tree. Now he was among the shadows of the Ho Bo Woods. There were Americans on either side of him. He could hear them pushing their way into the vegetation.

He was aware of the animals, the birds, and the lizards all around him. There was a scraping of tiny claws as something scurried up a tree.

"Hold it," said Morris. He stood there, turning his head right and left. The VC seemed to have vanished already.

Then, suddenly, a man yelled. "Here!" There was a burst of fire.

Morris ran toward the noise. He leaped over a log and dived for a bush. There was a flash of movement and he aimed at it but didn't fire. He didn't know who it was.

Keeping his rifle up, against his shoulder, he stared into the shadows. There was a *bloop* behind him as someone fired an M-79. He heard the round snap through the trees and threw himself to the ground as the grenade detonated. That was the problem with the M-79. After the grenade had spun so many times it would detonate against the slightest resistance.

"Hold the grenades," he ordered.

Up again, he forced his way deeper into the woods. There was a sergeant on his right who was fighting his way deeper. Morris caught movement again, but this time he could identify the target—a small man in black pajamas with an AK. Morris fired a short burst. The rounds tore through the woods, slamming into a tree near the man. He threw himself down, disappearing.

"Directly in front of you," called Morris.

"Saw him," yelled the sergeant. He kept his weapon high as he moved forward, trying to spot the man.

Morris heard someone firing to the right—AKs and M-16s on full auto—and then silence.

"We lose anyone?"

"No wounded," shouted one of the men.

Morris wiped a hand over his face and rubbed the sweat onto his jungle fatigues. He glanced right and left. There was a sergeant standing near him. He pointed forward, toward the area where the VC had fallen to cover. The sergeant nodded and slipped to his right.

Morris moved cautiously, his finger on the trigger of his M-16, the barrel pointed in the direction of the enemy. He stopped next to a small tree, leaning against the trunk of it. He tried to spot the enemy, but there was no movement.

Suddenly he was aware of the noise around him—his soldiers pushing on, into the forest. No one was firing now. No one was talking. They were hunting for the enemy, trying not to spook him, trying not to alert him—thirty Americans, searching for fewer than five VC.

The sergeant was now in position. Morris crouched and moved then, coming around a bush. He whipped his weapon around, pointing it at the spot where the VC soldier had been, but the ground was empty. Morris glanced at the sergeant, who shrugged.

Morris stepped forward, his weapon still at the ready. He could feel the sweat drip, tickling his sides and rolling down his back. It seemed hotter in the woods, as if they absorbed the heat rather than reflecting it.

He stopped for a moment. He then slipped to one knee and reached out, poking at the ground with his left hand. There was something wrong with the place. The bush didn't look quite right.

The ground seemed to explode in front of him. The bush lifted and flipped back. Without thinking, Morris dived to the right, flattening himself.

The sergeant fired a short burst and then two quick shots. There was a scream of pain and surprise. Morris rolled to the right, away from the bush, and squirmed around, aiming back at the bush.

The spider hole was apparent now. Morris stood up and moved toward it, looking down into it. The VC was slumped in the bottom, his face covered with his own blood, a neat hole between his eyes.

"Nice shooting, sergeant," said Morris.

"Wyatt Earp," said the sergeant. "Outdrew the fucker."

Morris handed his M-16 to the sergeant and then leaned down, grabbing the dead man by his shoulder and hauling him out of the hole. With the body out of the way, Morris found the AK, a pouch holding three spare magazines, and two Chicom grenades. There was nothing else in the hole and no way to get out of it—just a spider hole designed so that the man inside could ambush the Americans if he got the chance.

Shay appeared then. "I think we got them all. Four enemy KIA, not counting this one."

Morris checked the time. They had been on the ground for fifteen minutes. "Not bad," he said.

"What do we do now?"

"Drag the bodies back to the LZ so the fly-boys can confirm the dead. The men who killed them get the weapons."

"Yes, sir."

"And search the bodies for papers, maps, and unit insignia. Maybe our intelligence people can make something of it."

"Yes, sir."

As Shay headed off, Morris poked into the pockets of the dead man. He found nothing at all. The VC had followed the rules of sanitization. Carry nothing into the field that would be of benefit to the enemy.

Standing, he handed the AK and the pouch with the spare ammo to the sergeant. "Trophies of war."

"Thanks."

"I'd be careful with that ammo," said Morris. "I heard the Green Berets salt the area with dummy rounds designed to blow up."

"Great. I could get killed by our own people." The sergeant slung the AK and then draped the pouch with the spare magazines over his shoulder.

Together Morris and the sergeant dragged the body out of the trees. They pulled it over to where the other four were lying. Morris looked down at them and felt almost nothing at all. Here were five dead men, killed only minutes before, and he felt nothing. He didn't care because they weren't his soldiers. They were the enemy, and he didn't care that they had families and friends and wives. None of that mattered to him.

That was something that he had noticed. Unlike the movies where men were upset by their first kill, he was unaffected by it. Most of his soldiers had been unaffected by it. He didn't know if it was the cultural shock of being dragged halfway around the world, if it was the conditioning done by the army during basic training and AIT, or if there was something missing in the minds and spirits of the infantry soldiers. All he knew was that no one was upset by shooting a VC.

Shay was standing near him with a wallet in his hand. Morris asked, "What's that?"

"Only thing I could find on the bodies." Shay held up a slip of paper, a receipt of some kind. The asshole was in Saigon last night. At one of the bars."

"Turn that over to MI and let them worry about it."

"Them or the MPs," said Shay. "Maybe close the place down, just to irritate Charlie."

"Whatever." Morris slipped to the right to where the RTO was standing. He reached out for the handset. "Guess I'll whistle up the choppers and get us the hell out of here."

"Yes, sir," said the RTO. He hesitated and then added, "Looks like it worked."

For a moment Morris didn't know what he meant, and then realized he was talking about the Eagle Eye. They had swooped in, killed, and were now going to get the hell out of there.

"Yeah," he agreed. "I guess it did."

# ELEVEN

THE rest of the day was spent flying around in circles, returning to Cu Chi for fuel, and then getting airborne again. They just bored holes in the sky while Lead was off on a scouting mission, searching for the enemy.

Anderson had flown for a while, but tired of it. Flying formation wasn't easy. The pilot had to concentrate on the ship in front, making sure that he didn't fly too close, get too low, or fall back too far. And there were instruments to cross check. The pilot had to make sure that everything remained in the green, that the EGT didn't climb too high, and that the various fuel and hydraulic lines didn't spring leaks.

The real problem, Anderson realized, was that no one knew when anything was going to happen. They didn't know how long they would be airborne. All they knew was that they had to stay where they were, orbiting, orbiting, orbiting.

Although they were at two thousand feet, outside effective small-arms range, they were giving Charlie the perfect opportunity. If he could get a couple of .51-cals into the area, he could spend a few minutes setting up, aiming, and then have a field day hosing down the flight.

"Lead," said Anderson.

"Go."

"How about shifting us to the east or west by a couple of miles?"

"There a reason for that?"

"Roger. Keeps Charlie from getting a good shot at us."

"We're above AK range."

"The .51s are good to eleven thousand feet."

"Roger."

A moment passed, and then the original Lead came on the air. "Shift three klicks to the west and climb to three thousand feet."

"Roger."

Anderson sat back in his seat, happy with himself. He'd spotted a problem and had taken care of it. He put his foot up, bracing it in the corner of the console and the instrument panel. AFVN was still playing rock and roll, but the situation wasn't improving. He felt himself growing sleepy and wished that they could land for a few minutes. He needed to get out and stretch his legs, and to take a piss.

"You want to take it for a few minutes?" asked Nowlin.

"Nope."

"I need to relax."

Anderson shifted around, put his hands on the controls, and said, "I've got it."

"You've got it."

Anderson checked the instruments and then his position in the flight. He held it the best he could, staying with the aircraft in front of him. For a few moments, it was exciting, but then it became boring again—flying around and around with no destination and no idea how long it would be.

"Chock Two, say fuel status?" asked Lead.

"I'm down to about forty minutes."

"Roger. Head on to Dau Tieng to refuel."

"Roger. Will you be joining us there?"

"Negative. I'll be heading to Cu Chi. You remain at Dau Tieng until you hear from me again."

"Roger. Should we shut down?"

"Affirmative, but everyone stays with the aircraft. No raids on the PX or the club."

"Roger that."

The flight turned and headed to the northeast. The airfield at Dau Tieng was part of what had once been the plantation headquarters built by the French. There were a number of old buildings, stone and tile, and there was an above ground pool that was two stories tall and that still held water. Soldiers of the Twenty-fifth Infantry Division were sitting around the pool, sunning themselves.

The helicopters crossed the perimeter wire and headed on toward the POL. They landed there, but before their crews began refueling, the crew chiefs chased the grunts off the aircraft. This made sure that if one of the choppers blew up, the explosion wouldn't kill all the grunts.

While Anderson sat in the cockpit, the crew chief refueled. Anderson watched the fuel gauge slowly climb, until the aircraft had a full load. He held a thumb up, out the door, telling Brolin that they were finished.

Brolin put the nozzle back into the hunk of pipe and put the cap back on the fuel tank. He climbed into the cargo compartment and then waved at the grunts. They walked over slowly and got on board.

"Flight, let's move it off now. Wind them up."

The flight hovered back to the south and then lined up along the runway. Once the flight was situated, the order came through. "Let's shut them down. Three Seven, do you have Pounder Two Six?"

"Roger."

"Please let him know that we'll want everyone to remain with the aircraft."

"Roger that."

Over the intercom, Anderson said, "You got it."

"I've got it."

Turning in his seat, he saw Captain Morris kneeling on the deck near him. He waved the officer over and yelled over the dying noise of the turbine, "You'll need to keep your people close. I guess we can sit in the shade of the trees."

"I suppose a PX run is out of the question."

Anderson glanced across the runway to where the tiny PX sat. If they got the word to take off it would be four or five minutes before they could do it, even with everyone sitting on the aircraft. The helicopters had to be cranked. That would give the men in the PX plenty of time to get back.

"Couple of them at a time." said Anderson, "if they're listening for the sounds of us cranking. Why not?"

"I could have them bring you all a couple of Cokes."

"Well, then I would say there is plenty of time for a PX run."

The grunts climbed out of the aircraft and moved over to

where there was a line of trees. A revetment had been erected, designed to block the rotorwash and keep the swirling dust and debris from leaving the airfield. The grunts stripped their gear and stacked it there, leaning back against the metal of the revetment.

Anderson climbed out of the cockpit and walked around to the rear of the aircraft. He checked the tail boom, and then the rotor system, looking for bullet holes.

"We didn't take any hits," said Brolin, approaching from the right.

"I didn't think so either," said Anderson, "but I thought I'd better take a look anyway." He glanced at his watch. "You have any Cs?"

"Couple of meals in the back," said Brolin.

"I'll have to remember to tell Elway about that," said Anderson. He moved back and climbed up into the cargo compartment to fill out part of the book. He added up the flight time and found they had been airborne for almost seven hours. Army regulations said that no one was supposed to get more than eight hours in any one twenty-four-hour period.

Nowlin came around and got up on the troopseat. "Now what do we do?"

"We wait here." Anderson stuffed the log back into the map case and pulled a paperback out of his pocket. He waited for Nowlin to say more and, when he didn't, Anderson started to read. He kept at it, ignoring the sounds around him until Morris showed up with a can of Coke.

Anderson leaned over and took it and then sat back. Morris climbed up into the helicopter. He set his rifle on the deck and then took off his steel pot.

"Hot."

Anderson shrugged. "Always hot."

"How'd you think it went this morning?" Morris asked.

Anderson closed his book and said, "Let me turn that around on you. How do you think it went?"

Morris took a long pull at his Coke. "Went just fine. We took out five of the enemy with no one killed or wounded. Puts us up five to nothing."

"Is it worth it?" asked Anderson. "A lot of people involved in killing those five VC."

"Right now it's not cost effective," said Morris, "but then who ever said that fighting a war has to be cost effective? If that was an issue, there wouldn't be a war. You can't fight one and turn a profit."

"Colt Firearms and Bell Helicopter might argue the point," said Anderson.

"Now you're going in a different direction," said Morris. "I meant the actual fighting of it, not the manufacture of the goods used in that fighting."

"I understand that," said Anderson. He took a drink and said nothing else.

Morris finally asked, "What did you think of this morning's operation?"

"Well, Eagle Eye was designed to spot the enemy and engage him immediately, and we did do that. The question is, did we engage all of the enemy there or only the rear guard?"

"You think we should have pushed on?" asked Morris.

"No, sir," said Anderson. "I think you did exactly what you were supposed to do. Hit and run. If you had pressed on, who knows what you might have run into. Old cavalry tactics were to attack the rear guard of the column, or the flanks. Do as much damage as possible without exposing yourself to retaliation by the main body. We did that.''

"But you don't think much of it," said Morris.

"I think it's better than the search and destroy tactics of the infantry. It targets the enemy and not whoever happens to be sitting around."

Morris shrugged and finished his Coke.

At that moment, Gates moved out onto the runway and swung his arm around, telling them to crank. Anderson saw that and pointed it out.

"We're going again?"

"That's right."

Anderson finished the Coke quickly and tossed the can at Brolin. They couldn't throw cans out on the ground because the rotorwash would catch them and suck them up into the blades. As Brolin stored the can under his seat, Anderson climbed back into the cockpit.

Nowlin was strapping himself in. "What's going on?"

"How the hell should I know? We're just cranking them up." Glancing to the right, where the grunts were, Anderson could see Morris talking on the radio, learning a little more about the tactical situation.

As soon as the helicopters were at full operating RPM, the grunts swarmed aboard them. Anderson watched the flight load, saw that everyone was up and ready and keyed his mike. "You're loaded and ready to go."

"Roger. Coming up to a hover."

They took off, and turned to the south. Orbiting over the Song Sai Gon was the lone ship flown by Elway. He waited until the flight was approaching and then turned to the south.

"Four Five, do you have me in sight?"

"Roger that."

"Join on me."

"Roger."

As the flight came together, Anderson spotted the gunships down lower, racing along no more than ten or fifteen feet off the ground. He keyed the mike. "Lead, you're joined with all five aircraft."

"Rolling it over." There was a pause and then Lead said, "We have a squad spotted and are going to take them out. There is a village on the right there so we'll be operating under normal rules."

Anderson touched the intercom. "Got that Brolin? Fire for fire received."

"Roger."

They stayed near the river, now heading to the east, back toward Saigon. The ground below them was open, with fingers of woods reaching out as if to grab the river. There was smoke in one section of the woods—it looked like part of the Ho Bo Woods had caught fire.

"We're about two minutes out," Lead advised.

"Relay that to the grunts," said Anderson.

"Yes, sir."

In the distance Anderson saw the LZ. It was a group of rice paddies on the south side of a hamlet. He could see four or five hootches clustered in a stand of coconut and palm trees. South of them, maybe a hundred yards or so away, was a tree line, and behind that was a ditch.

The gunships stayed on the south side of the flight, twisting and turning to keep the tree line in front of them so they could fire on it if necessary.

The flight descended rapidly, the point in front of them a rice paddy filled with water. There was a farmer working it and, as the helicopters came in, his water buffalo suddenly took off running. The farmer held on for a moment, running after the beast, but then tripped, falling into the water. He was dragged a few feet and then let go as the buffalo leaped one dike and ran into another paddy.

Lead flared and dropped to the ground. Anderson hauled on the cyclic and dropped the collective at once. He came to a hover two feet above the water in the paddy. As he worked to set the aircraft on the ground, one of the grunts jumped. Anderson fought to keep the skids level. He set the aircraft on the ground, the water coming up over the skids.

The rest of the grunts jumped out and spread apart, moving toward the rice-paddy dikes. As they did, Anderson used the radio. "You're down with five and unloaded."

"Lead's on the go."

Anderson picked up to a hover as the rest of the flight took off. He dumped the nose and raced after them. "Lead, you're out with all five. Negative fire received."

# TWELVE

**M**ORRIS hit the water with a quiet splash and felt his foot sink into the muck at the bottom of the rice paddy. He could hear nothing but the roar of the turbines and the pop of the rotorblades. Water was caught up in the rotorwash and swirled around, stinging his face. He pulled at his foot and took a stumbling step forward, trying to get away from the noisy helicopter.

He reached the closest dike and knelt there, one knee against the mud. The remainder of his company was moving from the choppers toward the village. As they cleared the aircraft, the helicopters took off, and in moments it was quiet in the rice paddy.

Morris stood up and stepped over the short dike. He wanted to avoid them. Charlie mined the dikes, and the farmers usually knew where the booby traps were hidden, so they avoided them too. That meant soldiers tripped them.

The hamlet in front of him looked like a low island in the middle of a shallow lake. There was a single dike around it that kept the water from running into the hamlet. He could see two of the hootches, a short mud fence, a stand of palm and coconut trees, and a two-wheeled ox cart.

The soldiers moved, in line, toward the village. A couple hung back, watching the tree line. The others advanced slowly, moving through the rice paddies.

The farmer who had fallen as his ox ran off, stood up. Water dripped from his shirt and shorts. Mud was smeared on his head, matting down his hair. He didn't move as the soldiers approached him. Two broke out of the line and walked up to him. It was apparent that he had no weapons.

They continued to move forward. A kid ran from one hootch to another—a little kid who wore a black shirt but no pants, his, maybe her, bare bottom showing. It was impossible for them to tell whether it had been a little boy or a girl.

Morris reached another dike and stopped. Water had seeped into his boots and had soaked his pants to the knee. Sweat had stained his jacket. It had beaded on his face and was dripping down to the collar of his fatigue shirt. He reached up to wipe it away.

The sudden machine-gun burst came from the open door of the hootch. Morris saw the strobing of the muzzle flash before he heard the sound of firing. Water splashed around two of his men. One of them flipped back, sprawling in the rice paddy, losing his grip on his weapon. The other dived to the right with a flat splash, crawling up against the dike so that he would be invisible from the hamlet.

The whole company scattered, diving for cover. Morris

dropped into the water and pulled himself toward the corner of a rice-paddy dike. There was a rattling of M-16s as his men began to return the fire. An M-79 opened up, the grenade falling short. It detonated in the paddy, throwing up a fountain of water.

"Medic! We need a medic!"

Glancing to his right, Morris could tell that the man who had been hit was dead. His blood was spreading, staining the water, and he hadn't moved since he had been hit. Too much blood. Morris had seen men die before.

One of the M-60s began to pour fire into the enemy hootch. Ruby-colored tracers hit it, some bouncing high. Others flashed through the door. Smoke appeared in the thatch as flames began to eat away at it.

"Put out rounds," yelled Morris. Then he tried to spot his RTO. The man was crouched in another rice paddy. Morris was going to have to expose himself to get to the radio.

As the firing from his men increased, he leaped over the dike and landed flat. Water splashed up, into his face. He could smell it—filthy water filled with human waste.

"Movement in the east," yelled Shay.

Morris saw two men dressed in NVA green running through the middle of the hamlet. The ground under them began to boil as his soldiers shot at them. One man was hit, stumbled, but kept on running. The other took a burst in the back. It lifted him from his feet and threw him to the ground. He rolled once and didn't move again.

Now the first man was staggering. He had slowed but was still trying to reach the safety of a hootch. He was hit again, fell to his knees, and dropped his AK. He got back to his feet unsteadily and then fell against the mud wall, leaving a bloody smear there.

Morris reached the RTO. The man was crouched in the water, his head down, the antenna held in his right hand. He ignored Morris.

"I need to contact the guns."

For a moment the man didn't move. Then he let go of the antenna and reached around, pulling the handset out. "It's set on their freq."

Morris lifted it to his ear and said, "Five Nine, this is Pounder Two Six."

"Go Two Six."

"We are under fire from the hamlet. We have seen two civilians there and more than a dozen enemy including NVA. They have one machine gun and multiple automatic weapons. They are hidden in the hootches."

"Can you mark with smoke?"

"Negative. We are in the paddies to the south of the ville. Hit everything north of us."

"Roger."

Morris tossed the handset back to the RTO. He pulled his rifle around and aimed into the hamlet, but there were no targets for him. The firing there had tapered off, and the machine gun had stopped shooting.

The gunships roared in, circled to the west, and then made their first runs. The lead ship fired rockets at the hootches. Rockets slammed into the mud walls. A moment later there was an explosion. The roof lifted up and then collapsed back. Smoke poured out of the hootch as one of the walls fell. Flames began to spread in the thatch.

Inside there were four men. One tried to scramble from the hootch but was cut down by M-16 fire from the rice paddies. The others dived for cover. No one fired back at the gunship.

As the second ship rolled in, the enemy machine gun began to shoot. Green tracers flashed up at the helicopter. Morris pulled the trigger of his M-16, trying to hose down the enemy position, making them duck.

"Use the M-79," he ordered the men close to him. "Use the M-79."

There was a blooping sound, and the first of the grenades landed in the hamlet. Morris watched as the explosions walked toward the hootch. The machine gun fell silent.

With the gunships covering them the grunts began to move. Morris got up, leaped over the dike, and began splashing toward the hamlet. His soldiers were up and moving with him. They were firing from the hip. Tracers from the M-16s slammed into the mud hootches and the ox cart.

The water buffalo, enraged by the noise and the Americans, turned and attacked. It lowered its head and bellowing, leaped a dike. Two of the soldiers turned toward it. One shouted, but the animal kept coming. One man slipped to a knee, aimed, and emptied his whole magazine into the beast.

It didn't slow down, but the VC in the hamlet now opened fire. They were trying to hit the two Americans. Emerald-colored tracers flashed past them.

Neither paid attention to that. As the one man struggled to reload, the other, standing, opened fire. He aimed at the head, putting round after round into the animal. It began to slow, then staggered, and then toppled to its side. It kicked its legs a couple of times and then was still.

Both men whirled. One dived for cover in the rice paddy.

The other ran straight ahead, leaped a dike, and then jumped forward. He landed with a splash and pulled himself toward the dike.

Morris and some of the soldiers had reached the edge of the ville. Morris had taken cover behind the dike there. Peeking over the top, he could see into one of the hootches. In the shadows, one of the enemy soldiers moved.

The gunships kept flashing overhead, using their miniguns and rockets. The ground around Morris was being kicked up as if he were being shot at, but then he realized that it was the brass being kicked out by the guns.

Morris ignored the helicopters and fired into the hootch. The enemy soldier didn't react. He fired again and the man disappeared.

Shay reached him and said, "We've got four wounded now. Two dead."

"I think we've about got the ville taken. Once we can get the VC out, we can get a chopper in."

An RPD opened fire from a bunker at the side of a hootch. It was a dirt and log structure with only a small firing port that was just large enough to rake the rice paddies. The VC kept pouring fire out.

Morris tried to hit it with his M-16. He could see the rounds kicking up dirt all around the firing port. He emptied a magazine and then slipped back, his head below the level of the dike, so that he could reload.

"Hit the bunker," he called. "Everyone. Hit that fucking bunker."

As he spun around and looked, most of the men began to shoot. A cloud of dust drifted over the bunker. The men with the grenade launchers fired at it. Puffs of smoke and dust erupted all around it. The wall collapsed and the thatch of the roof slipped down, making it hard to see the enemy. But the muzzle flash set the grass on fire. As smoke obscured their view, Morris was up and moving again.

"There's movement on the right."

Morris dropped and spun. "Where?"

Shay was near him. "There. Four guys. Into that hootch right there."

"Put grenades on them."

Shay turned to go, took two steps, and his face exploded. He fell straight down and didn't move. Blood began to spread around him.

"Medic," yelled Morris, knowing that it would do no good. Shay was dead.

Firing erupted all around him. M-16s on full auto. AKs firing along with the RPDs. The detonations combined into a single, long explosion.

The RTO ran over and dropped to the ground. "I got the gunship pilot."

Morris took the handset. "This is Two Six."

"Roger, Two Six, we've got twenty, thirty people on the north side of the village running for the river."

"You'll have to take them. We're pinned down here for the moment."

"Roger that. Just wanted you to know what was happening up here."

Morris gave the handset back. He turned and crawled forward so that he was at the base of one of the trees. Rounds slammed into it, shaking it. Bits of bark and leaves rained down on him.

The grenadiers opened fire again. Four M-79s fired at the bunker. As those grenades detonated, a man ran forward, shoved a grenade through the firing port, and then leaped over the bunker. The grenade detonated with a muffled sound and smoke poured form the firing port.

"That's got it."

Morris was moving then, running through the village. He glanced in the open door of a hootch and saw a body lying sprawled. There was an AK near an outstretched hand. He thought about picking it up, but didn't. Instead he put a burst into the man's chest, making sure that he was dead. Turning, he leaped over a mud fence and then slowed.

The first of the gunships rolled in, again using the miniguns. The sound of the buzz saw cut through the air. The ground around the fleeing NVA boiled. Dust and smoke obscured them.

Morris raised his own weapon and fired single shots, selecting his targets carefully. He fired until the M-16 was empty. He ducked down, reloaded, and popped back up. Now the NVA had reached the river, and he could no longer see them. He waited for a moment, watched the gunships continue to fire, and then got back to his feet.

Returning to the center of the hamlet, he found the medic working on a wounded soldier. The man sat on the ground, his fatigue jacket next to him. The medic was tying a bandage around his upper arm.

"We'll want to get him back to Cu Chi," said the medic without looking up.

"As soon as we can."

Morris spotted the RTO standing near the ox cart. One of the sergeants was near him. A couple of men were bringing the body of a dead man out of the rice paddies. Morris wished Shay was around so that he could talk to him. He wished Shay wasn't dead. He wished that he'd never heard of Eagle Eye.

"We've got four dead and seven wounded," said the sergeant. "Should get the wounded evacced as soon as we can."

"We'll need a body count on the NVA, plus weapons and documents."

"Yes, sir. Got the people working on it now. I also made sure that security was out."

"Yeah," said Morris. "I should have been thinking of that myself, but I saw the enemy getting out."

"How many?"

"At least thirty. That force was the same size as ours."

"Then why'd they run? They had all the advantages," said the sergeant.

"Except for mobility. They couldn't get reinforcements and we could. They knew that, so they got out."

"Yes, sir."

"You find the villagers yet?"

"No, sir. Haven't seen a civilian yet."

"They're probably hiding from us." Morris shook his head. "Always hide from us."

"Yes, sir."

Morris looked around for a moment. He could see the bodies of the NVA scattered through the hamlet. Ten or twelve of them were visible now. His soldiers were dragging others out, into the open.

He stood there, listening as the gunships made their last run on the enemy. He watched them fly over the top of the ville. The RTO appeared, and Morris reached for the handset.

"Blackhawk Four Five, this is Pounder Two Six."

"Go."

"We are ready for extraction. Be advised that we'll need two ships for medevac."

"Roger that."

He gave the handset back to the RTO and said, "Maybe this isn't such a great idea after all."

"It's put us in contact with the enemy twice in one day," the RTO said. "That's something that doesn't normally happen."

"No." said Morris. He walked over to where the body of Shay lay facedown. Someone had covered his head with an olive drab towel that was already soaked in blood. Flies were thick around him, their buzzing now sounding louder than the firing of the miniguns or the turbines of the choppers.

Crouching there, near the body of his friend, Morris wanted to say or do something but didn't know what. All he could do was keep the flies and the enemy away. That was all that was left to do.

# THIRTEEN

**E**LWAY called the meeting and asked that Morris be there. He also wanted Nichols there. It was for all the officers involved in the Eagle Eye project, and he placed guards around his tent so that the Vietnamese couldn't sneak in close to listen. Elway was convinced that there were Viet Cong in the camp. He'd heard too many stories about ARVN soldiers and Vietnamese workers in American camps who eventually revealed their true colors and led attacks on those very camps.

Anderson was not happy with the situation. He figured they should head back to Cu Chi and discuss things with Fox and the infantry there. But Elway wanted to keep things close to home, figuring they could devise solutions if they thought about it just a little bit.

Elway sent one of the door gunners out to find Cokes or

beer for the officers and, as the crewman disappeared, Elway said, "I think things went fairly well today."

Morris didn't respond right away. He still wore his sweat-and-rice-paddy-stained fatigues. He had kept his M-16 in his hand. He sat on the wooden floor of the tent. "I think we were lucky we didn't get the shit kicked out of us."

"Maybe we'd better discuss the results of the afternoon mission first," Elway said. "Mister Nichols?"

Nichols didn't move. He sat on a footlocker. In a low voice he said, "We caught them on the southern bank of the river. There were a couple of sampans there, and they were trying to escape in them. We hosed down the area."

He looked up. "It was like shooting fish in a barrel. They didn't know what hit them. One minute they're in the hamlet and the next they're running for their lives. Our miniguns and door guns took them out because they didn't have any cover. I counted forty-two bodies on the bank and in the water, and I didn't try very hard to count them."

"Jesus," said Morris. "What'd we run into?"

Elway said, "Looks like a company, at least. What was the body count in the hamlet?"

"We found nineteen in the hamlet, seven in a bunker, and there were twelve in the rice paddy behind the hamlet. I think most of those were killed by the gunships, and they should get credit for them."

"Shit," said Nichols.

"What's your problem?" asked Elway.

"For one thing, you're talking about human beings. We killed what, seventy, seventy-five people, and you're talking about taking credit for it. If we were back in the World, there would be police all over the place.''

Elway stared at the man.

''Think about it this way,'' said Nichols. ''In the World, the police surround a building, there's a little shooting, and then the bad guys surrender. Here, everyone opens fire with everything they have trying to actively kill one another. No one comes out with his hands up. Just everyone killing everyone else.''

''Which is our job,'' said Elway.

Nichols rubbed a hand over his face. ''I'm not making my point. I just find it grotesque that the way we measure progress in this war is by the number of bodies we can pile up. There is something very sick about it.''

''Maybe you'd like to return to the slick platoon,'' said Elway.

''Don't go jerking my chain,'' said Nichols. ''I'm just telling you this is a sick thing and I don't have to be thrilled with the idea of hosing down a bunch of men on the bank of a river. It wasn't even much of a firefight. They were too scared to shoot back at us.''

''Then you should have captured them,'' said Elway sarcastically.

''Right. I could land and load them in the rear of my gunship.''

Anderson spoke up then. ''This is getting us nowhere.''

''Anderson's right,'' said Elway.

''I just thought someone ought to point out that human lives were involved in this contest,'' said Nichols. ''It's not like we're raising our production quota for the betterment of the human race.''

''That point's debatable too,'' said Anderson. He caught

the look on Nichols' face. "I mean, the elimination of communism might actually be better for the human race."

"You know what I mean," said Nichols.

"Yeah," said Anderson, quietly, "I do."

Morris took advantage of the lull in the conversation. "Near as I can figure now, we were outnumbered, what, two to one. The enemy was equipped with AKs, RPDs, but no RPGs. We landed in an open field and could have had the shit shot out of us before anyone could get in to help."

Elway scratched the side of his head, nodding. "We need to coordinate this a little better."

"Rather than orbiting," said Morris, "maybe you could get back here to pick up the second lift. That way, if we need help, it can get there as quickly as possible."

"Unless you need to be extracted," said Elway. "Then we're fully loaded and have to land somewhere to get rid of the troops in the back."

Morris shook his head. "Then maybe the size of the landing force is too small."

"The concept says that we need small units ready to attack the enemy where we find him. Hit and run. We can't have ten aircraft airborne."

"Why the hell not?" asked Morris. "Isn't the whole point of this to find the enemy? Right now, the aviation companies are scheduled to fly the troops from point A to point B, let them off, and then fly somewhere else. What's the point of that? Why, we're searching for the enemy, which is exactly the same thing that they're doing. The difference is we don't land until we find the enemy."

"There are good reasons for search and destroy missions," said Elway.

Morris grinned. "You can say that because you aren't on the ground walking around."

"Weapons caches," said Elway. "An armed force seen by the people is a deterrent to leanings toward the enemy."

"Oh, bullshit," said Morris. "The civilians have already made up their minds about this. They either support the VC and NVA or they don't. We plunder through a couple of neutral villes, shoot a couple of pigs, knock down a couple of walls, and suddenly the people aren't neutral anymore. They're supporters of the VC."

"We are getting off the subject here," said Elway. "We should confine our comments to the missions flown."

"Why?" asked Morris. "Because you know I'm right."

"No. I just think that we need to give this a chance to work," said Elway.

"The concept is good," said Anderson suddenly. "Hit the enemy and get out. Forget the crap about winning hearts and minds. Forget the propaganda aspects. Get out and kill the enemy."

"Easy for you to say," said Nichols. "You haven't had to pull the trigger."

"Which isn't to say I wouldn't," said Anderson.

"How do you know, before you have to do it?" asked Nichols quietly.

"I've thought my way through that question and I know the answer. As long as it is an enemy soldier who is armed and ready to fight, I have no qualms about pulling the trigger. Opening fire on a village where we suspect there are enemy soldiers but don't know. . . that's another question all together."

"Gentlemen," said Elway, "we've gotten off the topic."

"No," said Morris, "we're right on it. There are people

who can spend their tours in Vietnam and never have to fire their weapons. Given the way some of these units operate, they avoid contact more often than make it. We're out there searching, actively searching for the enemy. We're not poking into suspected VC strongholds or weapons caches. We're not landing unless there are armed enemy soldiers on the ground. We need to know each other's feelings.'' Morris looked at Nichols.

"Don't worry about me,'' said Nichols. "I'll do my job. I'll do it very well, but I don't have to be thrilled with the idea of killing people. Besides, at this point, it's too late to worry about it. I killed ten or twenty people today.'' He was quiet for a moment and then added, "I don't have to like it, but I am very good at it.''

Elway again tried to take charge of the meeting. He said, "Are there any recommendations about how to coordinate or improve this activity?''

"I'd like the helicopters standing by as close as they can. We lucked out today because Charlie didn't stand and fight. If he had, we'd have been chopped up in the rice paddies.''

"Maybe,'' said Anderson, "that was a result of previous operations. Charlie knows that where there are five helicopters, there are probably a dozen more. He knows that we'll keep bringing in soldiers and there will be gunships and artillery. I might point out that was an option today.''

"No,'' said Morris. "Artillery was not an option today. We had seen civilians in the village. We couldn't call in artillery until we knew they were clear.''

"Did they get clear?'' asked Anderson.

"No,'' said Morris, shaking his head. "Six civilians were killed.''

"By whom?'' asked Elway.

"Does it really matter?" asked Morris. "They're dead no matter who killed them, and the point can be made that if we hadn't attacked the enemy where we did, they wouldn't have died, so you can say we killed them whether it was done by our bullets or our actions."

Elway looked at the man and then shook his head. Everyone seemed to be worried about the deaths of the Vietnamese. First Nichols, shooting his mouth off about the deaths of the VC on the banks of the river, and now Morris, ready to take the blame for the villagers. These were discussions that he didn't want to get into. His orders were clear—fly out in search of the enemy and kill him wherever he was found.

"Recommendations," said Elway finally.

"All right," said Morris. "I'd like our recons to be a little tighter. I'd like a better idea of what we're landing in before we do it."

"We spend too much time over the target and we're going to tip off the enemy," said Elway.

"Not to mention getting the shit shot out of us," said Anderson.

"Seems to me," said Morris, "that a poor recon is going to result in you getting the shit shot out of you anyway when you land to pick up the remains of my unit."

"That could happen," said Anderson. "I meant that if we give Charlie more than a ten-second look at us, we're giving him all the time he needs to shoot us out of the sky. You have to remember that the life expectancy of a helicopter pilot in combat is less than thirty seconds."

"What the hell does that mean?" asked Morris.

"It means that in a combat environment, with Charlie firing at the flight, a pilot, sitting in his world of Plexiglas, up there without a gun in his hand but only a cyclic and collective, can expect to live about thirty seconds. That is in a hot LZ with Charlie there.''

''Then it is incumbent on all of us to do this in the best fashion possible,'' said Morris.

''Which brings me back to the original question,'' said Elway. ''Recommendations.''

''I just want us to have better intelligence before we land,'' said Morris. ''Maybe you should stick one of your helmets on one of my sergeants as you scout around. He can be searching out the infantry aspects of this while you all look at the aviation end of it.''

''That we can do,'' said Elway.

''And I'd like one of the choppers hanging close for evacuation of wounded or as a spotter for artillery if we should need it.''

Elway looked at Anderson and grinned. ''Sounds like a job for Trail.''

''Certainly,'' said Anderson. ''Except that cuts your aircraft by one-fifth.''

''If we need to bring in the second lift, we can split the load up. By the time the second lift comes in we'll have burned off enough fuel.''

''Okay,'' said Anderson. ''I can circle over the battle. But, if I have to land, for whatever reason, I'm going to need gunship cover.''

Nichols nodded and said, ''That'll make a coordination problem. Do I expend, or do I hold some of it back in case Trail has to make a heroic, medal-earning landing while we cover his ass?''

''What's the turnaround on rearming?'' asked Morris.

"Forty, forty-five minutes, if we're lucky and if there is no one else waiting to rearm."

"Hell," said Anderson, "we can't sit here and figure out a policy that's going to work. Each situation is going to be different."

"Then I use my best judgment," said Nichols.

"Exactly," said Elway. He took a deep breath. Now he was beginning to look bored. "Anything else?"

"I need to head into Cu Chi to rearm," Nichols said.

"Couldn't that wait until morning?" asked Elway.

"Could," said Nichols, "but what the hell good is an unarmed gunship? If Charlie hits here tonight, I'll be as useless as tits on a boar."

"Go after dinner," said Elway.

"I'd rather go now, while we've got some light. Makes the task easier."

"As soon as we break up here, you've got an hour," said Elway.

"I said we could rearm in forty-five minutes under ideal conditions and rushing to get it done. I don't see a need to do that now."

"Then take whatever time you need," said Elway.

"And I'd like to take Anderson with me."

"What the hell for?"

"Well, it doesn't hurt to have a couple of other people along knowing how to assist us. Little on-the-job training for him. You can never tell when that's going to help."

"Fine," said Elway. "Take him with you. Now, how long do you think it'll be before you can get back?"

"Well, since we're going into Cu Chi, I probably should have maintenance take a quick look at a couple of minor problems, and while we're there, I could get a couple of cases of Coke and beer from the club to bring back for the troops.''

''Fine,'' said Elway, realizing that he was being snowed. ''How long?''

''Well, if we're not back by midnight, I'd start sending out the search parties.''

''Midnight,'' said Elway.

''The witching hour,'' said Nichols. ''Should be back before then. Easily.''

# FOURTEEN

"**T**HAT didn't take forty-five minutes," said Anderson as he climbed into the rear of the helicopter.

"But that's only because we didn't have to load forty-eight rocket pods or the three hundred grenades like we would have if we'd had those weapons systems. Our biggest trouble is laying the M-60 ammo in there so that there are no kinks in the chain," said Nichols. "Otherwise it could easily take forty-five minutes. Besides, if Elway thinks we can do it faster, he's going to want it done faster and there could come a time when we physically couldn't do it."

"So now where are we going?" asked Anderson.

"Well, Andy, I would think that we've earned ourselves a round at the Gunfighter's Club. No reason that we can't head on down there for a drink or two."

"Except Elway is expecting us back."

"Not before midnight," said Nichols, grinning broadly.

"Okay," Anderson said. "I just wanted to make sure you had thought your way through this."

"Then you're not turning down the trip into Saigon?" asked Nichols.

"Hell, no." Anderson sat down on the deck and waited until the crew chief had put the troopseat back into place over the chutes designed to carry the ammo to the miniguns. He noticed that someone had stuck a screwdriver between the barrels so that they couldn't be turned by hand. If someone did that, the gun would begin to fire.

Nichols and Craig crawled into the cockpit. The crew chief pulled the screwdriver out and then sat down next to Anderson. Nichols started the aircraft, ran it up, and then picked it up to a hover. They held there for a moment, rocking gently in the ground effect, only a foot or so up, and then began to slip forward.

"Nearly overloaded," the crew chief shouted.

Anderson nodded. He understood that. The gunships, when they had a full load of fuel and a full load of ammo, pushed the limits of the operating envelope. Sometimes they were so heavy that the only way to get airborne was with a running takeoff. The pilot would kick the pedals back and forth to break them free, and then push the cyclic forward slowly so that the aircraft would begin to move. It was like taking off in an airplane. Once transitional lift was hit, the aircraft could leave the ground and build up more airspeed.

They hovered forward, passed the POL points, and then began to climb out, over the wire to the north. Anderson could see the dark shapes of the men as they moved into the bunker area for guard duty that night. Each of the bunkers would be manned in the off chance that Charlie would attempt an assault on the base camp. It had been nearly fourteen months since he had even probed the perimeter.

They turned toward Saigon, and Anderson leaned back to enjoy the ride. He'd spent quite a bit of time riding in the back now, and it was better than flying it himself. No worries. Just hang on and don't fall out.

They landed at Hotel Three and shut down. Nichols shut the doors on the cargo compartment, and the crew chief stuck screwdrivers in between the barrels of the miniguns. They then walked off the heliport and down the road and passed the World's Largest PX.

They followed the giant green footprints to the front door of the Gunfighter's Club. The guard glanced at them to make sure they were rated and let them pass. They entered and then stopped close to the lockboxes.

Over the din of rock and roll, Anderson said, "Now we've got until midnight."

"I said we'd be back by midnight. We should get out of here by eleven-thirty, then," said Anderson.

"You got something going already?" asked Nichols.

"Nope. I'm just not going to get caught short like I did the last time."

"Then head on in," said Nichols.

Anderson did as he was told and then shook his head. Nothing ever changed in the club. There was a naked woman dancing on the stage, there were pilots three deep at the foot of it waving money at her, and there were dozens of others drinking as fast as they could. The air force pilots were yelling at the army pilots, who were yelling at the navy pilots. The navy pilots were doing carrier landings on two tables moved together—they were slinging people belly first onto them while two men on either side tried to catch the belts of the men as they slipped by. Those men were the arresting gear.

"Kids," said Nichols, shaking his head. "Just a bunch of little kids."

"We going to drink?" asked Craig.

"Now that you mention it," said Nichols, "you can get us all a beer apiece. We'll press on and see if we can capture a table."

Anderson stood up on his tiptoes and searched the crowd slowly. There were some women sprinkled in among the men. Most of them were in dresses, though a couple were wearing fatigues. He thought he recognized one or two of them, but Sandy wasn't among them.

Nichols slapped him on the arm and dragged him into the crowd. There was a table with two men sitting at it. Nichols said, "I went to flight school with these guys, and we can join them."

Anderson pulled out a chair and dropped into it. Nichols introduced the men, but Anderson didn't hear their names, and he didn't care. The odds were that he would never see them again. All he was interested in was searching for Sandy.

Craig arrived with three beers. He set them on the table, found a chair, and sat down. He turned so that he could watch the dancer.

"This is getting old," said Anderson.

"It's better than sitting in a bunker waiting for the Vietcong to overrun the perimeter." Nichols took a long pull at his beer.

Anderson turned and saw Sandy walk into the club. She

was with two other women, and before they got halfway to the bar they were surrounded by men.

"Catch you later," said Anderson. He drained his beer and set the bottle down.

He moved through the crowd, managed to shove his way closer to her, and called, "Hey, Sandy."

She turned toward him, saw him, and grinned. "You made it down tonight."

"For a while," he said.

She separated herself from the group and moved closer to him. She reached down and grabbed his hand. "You going to be here all night?"

"Nope. Just until about eleven or so. Then we've got to head back."

"What are you doing?"

Anderson hesitated, wanting to tell her about Eagle Eye, but only because it was a plan that had grown out of his idea. But that was the war, and he didn't want to talk about the war. So he said, simply, "Flying. Everyday."

"You want to stay here?" she asked.

Anderson shot a glance over his shoulder at the girl dancing, at the men yelling at her, and then at the table where Nichols and his friends sat. It was noisy and hot and smoky. It was hard to breath.

"Where did you want to go?"

"Out," she said.

"Sure," said Anderson.

They walked back through the entry, and Anderson opened the door. As usual, Anderson expected it to be more comfortable outside, but it was hot and humid out there too. They walked down the road, away from the guard.

"We could get a taxi and head downtown," she said.

Anderson shook his head. "There's no time."

"There never is," said Sandy.

"It's not my fault."

"I know." She reached up and touched his cheek. "It's strange. The men assigned here are always talking about how rough it is, but you never mention it. You just get in once in a while. Not very often."

"And I'm lucky to be here tonight. I should be back at the camp. We needed to rearm one of the helicopters, so we used it as an excuse to get into here."

She looked around. There were a couple of barracks, their ground floors hidden behind sandbags, some of their windows boarded up. There were lights on in them. To the right was a long, low building that probably housed offices or supply sheds.

"No where for us to go," she said.

"Kind of like teenagers without a car. No place for us to be alone." As he spoke, he realized the irony of the statement, because he was a teenager. He was out of high school, but he was a teenager. He'd meant the kids still in school who lived at home and didn't have a place of their own.

"We could walk," she said.

"Fine," said Anderson. He glanced at his watch. He still had a couple of hours.

"My place is downtown," she said. "A taxi ride and we'll be at my room."

Anderson felt his stomach turn over. He wanted to do it—head downtown to her room and forget about the ride back to the ARVN camp—but the arguments against it were the same as they had been last time.

"I think," he said, "that we'd better just go back into the club."

"If that's what you want," she said.

"No, but it's the only course that makes sense now." He hesitated and said, "I'm sorry. There's nothing I can do about it."

"I'm sorry too," she said.


At eleven, Anderson found Nichols still sitting at the table, but now with a Coke in front of him. Anderson was still holding hands with Sandy. They had been dancing, and he was now bathed in sweat. His wet hair hung down as if he had just come from the shower.

"Christ," yelled Nichols, "what have you been doing?"

Anderson ignored the question. "We're going to have to get going."

Nichols checked the time and nodded. "Let me finish this first, and we'll go."

A moment later, he slammed his empty can to the table and stood up. "Gentlemen," he said, "it's been real, but I've got to get back to the field to crush communism."

"We all do that," said one of the men.

"But we do it better," said Nichols. "We do it out in the field and not here in Saigon."

"You might do it better," conceded the man, "but we do it in more comfort."

Nichols bowed and said, "I bow to your better thought." To Anderson and Craig, he said, "Let's get out of here."

Anderson turned to Sandy. "Next time I'm in, I'll call you."

"Next time make sure that you can spend more time here," she said.

"Yes, ma'am," said Anderson. He leaned forward and kissed her. Then, without waiting, he whirled and headed for the doorway.

Outside, Nichols shook his head. "I don't understand it. What could she possibly see in you?"

"I'm polite, I don't spit on the floor, and I can carry on a conversation."

"Who wants to talk?" asked Craig.

"Well, there you have it," said Anderson. "Now you know. Sometimes the woman likes to talk, and you have to be able to do it. Your attitude does you in."

They walked along the fence at the edge of the heliport. There were only two helicopters parked there now. The terminal under the tower was dark. No passengers waiting to get out into the field, out to the base camps, and out into the other areas in Vietnam.

Anderson climbed into the rear of the helicopter and waited as Nichols and Craig worked their way through the run-up procedures. He closed his eyes, thinking about Sandy, about dancing with her, about the things she had been whispering, some of them lost in the noise of the club. But he had heard enough to know what she'd been trying to do. She had done it quite well. He tried to put it out of his mind by opening his eyes and staring out through the windshield.

They flew on for a while, Anderson isolated by the darkness and the noise. Nichols and Craig were up front, where they were now nothing more than vague shapes outlined in the red from the instrument panel. The crew chief was sitting on the edge of the troopseat, looking down into the blackness of the Vietnamese landscape.

Far in front of them he saw a number of flares hanging in the air. There were points of light in the distance. As one of them winked out another appeared. As he watched, a line of tracers flashed upward.

Craig turned around and yelled, "Looks like they're hitting our camp."

He sounded calm about it. Anderson slipped to the left and stared out. Now he could see muzzle flashes twinkling on the ground, a dozen or more of them. Ruby-colored tracers streaked and struck the ground, tumbling.

Anderson moved forward, one knee on the rough metal of the deck. Nichols turned to the south and began a tight orbit. Anderson shouted, "What are you going to do?"

Nichols held up a hand, and Anderson could see that he was talking on the radio. Below, he could see the shapes of the enemy moving toward the camp—not many of them, running across the open ground, firing their weapons.

The crew chief touched Anderson on the shoulder. "Can you man the other machine gun?"

"What?"

"The other M-60. Can you handle it?"

"Yeah." Anderson had watched as the door gunners had mounted the machine guns on the slicks more than once. He knew how to load them—except these weren't mounted but on bungee cords.

Anderson moved back and picked up the M-60. He opened the top, laid in a belt of linked ammo and pulled back on the bolt. The crew chief said, "Careful that you don't put rounds through the rotors on the break. Don't track too far and don't shoot holes in the skids. Just try to cover on the break."

"Got it," yelled Anderson.

"Take the spare helmet."

Anderson set the machine gun down and put on the helmet. He heard Nichols say, "We'll make one pass and keep right on going. If we have to, we'll make a second pass later."

"Okay," said Anderson.

They turned around, heading back to the north. They dropped down lower, the helicopter's nose pointed at the men running across the ground, heading for the wire. The miniguns fired once, a burst of less than a second. The interior of the chopper lighted up like it had burst into flame. The muzzle flash was eight feet long and the tracers reached out like a red ray, dancing across the open ground.

The enemy soldiers stopped running almost as if commanded. They turned, firing back at the chopper. Their green tracers came up, flashing past it. Nichols touched the triggers again and the miniguns fired. The bullets slammed into the ground. Tracers tumbled into the sky. The firing from the enemy slowed and then stopped.

The gunship broke then, pulling up as Nichols turned it. Anderson leaned out, the stock of the M-60 up on his shoulder. He pulled the trigger and the weapon fired. The belt of ammo jerked past him rapidly. Spent cartridges bounced off the soundproofing and hit the floor.

Anderson saw one man on the ground. A dark shape. He walked the tracers toward it, watching it, trying to kill it and suddenly realized that if he kept firing he would shoot up the cockpit.

"Coming around again," said Nichols.

But now the enemy was trying to get out. The ruby tracers from the bunker line were flashing. The bunker line was twinkling like woods filled with fireflies in the summer. There were detonations sprinkled around—M-79 grenades exploding among the fleeing enemy soldiers.

"One more pass," said Nichols.

Flares burst into brilliance then. The enemy soldiers were now highlighted. Anderson leaned forward and fired with his M-60. Nichols lined up and fired the miniguns. The ground around the enemy churned under the impact of the rounds. Anderson closed his eyes to avoid the muzzle flashes. The weapon roared, drowning out the sound of the turbine and the rotors.

When he looked again there was no movement on the ground. He could see a couple of bodies, ripped apart under the hail of bullets. Firing from the bunker line had ceased, and there was none incoming.

Over the intercom, Nichols said, "That broke their back. We're heading on in."

Anderson sat back, opened the top of the M-60, and cleared the linked ammo from it. He worked the bolt, making sure that there wasn't a round chambered. Carefully, he set the weapon on the deck at his feet. Finally he looked at the crew chief and said, "Wow."

"Quite impressive," the chief agreed.

Impressive wasn't the word. Anderson hoped that he would never be on the receiving end. There was no way to survive in a world where the rounds were coming down at better than six thousand a minute. It would be thicker than the rain in a monsoon and certainly more deadly. If they could have carried more ammo, the enemy would never be able to survive. Six thousand rounds weighed a great deal.

"Wow," said Anderson again. He could think of nothing else that fit.

# FIFTEEN

A S they landed, Nichols said, "I'm going to have to rearm again."

"Maybe you should wait until morning this time," said Anderson.

"Maybe we should see what Elway's going to do. The flight should be cranked and ready to lift off," said the chief.

"Maybe you should go tell him we're back now," said Nichols.

Anderson stripped his flight helmet off and dropped it back to the deck. He leaped out of the helicopter and ran between the hootches, toward the tents where the pilots lived. The area was almost deserted, and he realized that he didn't know where Elway and the others would go during a ground attack. He figured that the grunts would head for the bunker line. Adding fifty or sixty weapons to it would surprise and demoralize the attacking enemy soldiers.

He stood for a moment and then turned, walking back the way he'd come. During an assault, the pilots should have been trying to get airborne, to get the aircraft off the ground so that the enemy couldn't destroy them. Apparently Elway hadn't thought of that.

He spotted Clarke moving toward the aircraft. Anderson walked up to him. "Where is everyone?"

"Bunkers over there," said Clarke, pointing.

"Elway with them?"

"Yeah. He was the first one to get there when the probe started."

"Should have been trying to get the aircraft out of here," said Anderson.

"The suggestion was made, but by then everyone was in the bunker and there was a hell of a lot of shooting. We decided we'd better stay where we were."

"Yeah. Maybe we should get airborne now and see if we can chase down the enemy."

"Elway's still in the bunker."

Anderson moved across the compound, around the hootches the Americans who lived at the camp used, to a series of small bunkers. He crouched in the entrance to one of them. "Lieutenant Elway? You in there?"

"What do you want?" came a voice.

"I think we'd better get the flight airborne," said Anderson.

"I think we'd better be staying right here."

Anderson scratched the back of his head and then said, evenly, "I believe that our function is to search out the enemy and attack him. The enemy is just beyond the wire. I think we'd better go get him."

There was a momentary silence, and then one of the other pilots said, "Anderson's right."

"It'll be impossible to see the enemy in the dark," said Elway.

"Difficult certainly," said Anderson. "Not impossible. Besides, this is what I was talking about. Charlie moves at night. We should move at night too. If nothing else, we'll irritate him."

Elway suddenly appeared in the door of the bunker. "I don't like you upstaging me," he said, his voice low. "You're only a warrant officer."

"Better than a lieutenant," said Anderson. "At least I know what the hell I'm doing."

Elway forced his way out of the bunker and stood there, his hands on his hips. "I'm going to report your behavior to Major Fox at the first opportunity."

Anderson had to laugh. "Go ahead. And be sure to tell him that while you were hiding in the bunker, I, along with Nichols and Craig, was shooting it out with the enemy who was attacking the camp. That'll make you look real good— make you into a real hero."

Ignoring that, Elway said, "I don't like this grandstand play either."

"Our job," said Anderson, "is to engage the enemy and not hide in the bunkers."

For a moment it looked as if Elway was going to strike Anderson. Finally he said, "I don't know where the grunts are now."

"On the bunker line, for Christ's sake. Let's get airborne while we can still accomplish something."

Elway turned, ducked, and yelled back into the bunker, "Let's hit the flight line." He stood and, without a word, pushed past Anderson.

Nowlin came up and said, "Thanks a lot. I thought I was going to get to hide down here the rest of the night."

"That really what you wanted to do?" asked Anderson. He started toward the flight line.

Staying with him, Nowlin said, "No. But, hell, it wasn't my decision to head here."

"Even if we weren't involved in this Eagle Eye thing," said Anderson, "it just makes good sense to get the aircraft off the ground. Hell, they're sitting out there where the enemy could hose them down if he wanted."

Nowlin turned back toward the tents. "Well, if I'm going to fly, I better get my helmet and my weapon."

"Good, God," said Anderson. "You didn't take a weapon to the bunker?"

"Why should I?"

"Just suppose, for the sake of argument, that the defense on the bunker line collapsed. What were you going to do? Call time out?"

"We never take weapons at Cu Chi."

"This isn't Cu Chi. At Cu Chi, they're what, ten thousand American soldiers for the defense? Here there are fewer than a thousand, and most of them are Vietnamese."

"I wasn't thinking."

"Nobody was. Christ, when the shooting started, you should have been getting the helicopters into the air before the enemy got a chance at them."

"Elway didn't say anything."

Anderson shook his head. "You can't trust lieutenants. They're all real live officers. They're into their careers and looking good for the brass and not rocking the boat. We have to think for them.''

They walked back to the tent area. Anderson opened his footlocker and took out his M-16 and a bandolier of ammo. He stared down at his pistol and then picked it up. Sometimes a pistol was a better weapon than an M-16. There were times when only a pistol would do. He also took out his helmet and a survival knife and he thought about the first-aid kit. Each helicopter had two of them attached to the bulkheads. The crew chief and door gunners had to make sure they weren't stolen by the passengers.

Anderson strapped on the pistol, slung the rifle, and stepped back out, into the night. He was suddenly aware of everything around him. The shadows were swinging because the flares above them were swinging under their parachutes. The firing had died out. In the distance, artillery boomed.

As Anderson reached the parking area, he saw that the grunts were beginning to move among the aircraft. They were dressed in fatigues and wearing their steel pots. They carried their weapons and spare ammo. One man had a radio.

Anderson opened the door of his aircraft and stood there for a moment. Elway was now at the lead helicopter and talking to two of the grunts. In the eerie light of the flares, Anderson could make that out easily.

Nowlin opened the door on the other side. ''Do we preflight?''

''Let's walk around the outside and make sure there are no bullet holes.'' Anderson crouched and looked under the Huey, searching for signs of a fuel leak. Standing, he moved along the side and back to the tail boom, running a hand along the smooth, cool metal. No sign of combat damage.

As he turned, he saw a light flash in front of him. A pilot was up on top of his aircraft, using his flashlight to check the blades for damage. Anderson stared at the blades on his own aircraft. There was nothing there to see.

"We ready?" asked Nowlin.

Anderson nodded. He walked to the rear so that he could grab the hook that was up through the end of the rotorblade, holding it tied to the tail boom. He unfastened it, swung the blade out, and then unhooked it.

Two of the grunts climbed into the rear of his helicopter. Anderson was going to say something to them about that but decided against it. They were probably safer there than standing off to the side.

Anderson returned to the cockpit, got in, but left the door standing open. He reached over and flipped on the battery switch and the start fuel. He checked to make sure the start generator was engaged. Leaning to the right, he used the other collective to set the throttle just below the flight idle detent, and then sat up.

"What are we waiting for?" asked Nowlin.

"Lead."

The rotating beacon on the lead aircraft began to flash. The rear of the turbine began to glow as the rotor started to turn slowly.

"That's got it," said Anderson. He turned in his seat and asked, "Are we clear?"

"Clear!" shouted the crew chief.

Anderson turned on the rotating beacon, glanced around, and then yelled, "Clear!" He leaned over and pulled the trigger under the collective next to the right seat.

When the turbine was fired and operating, he let go of the trigger, hesitated, and then rolled the throttle over the flight idle detent.

Sitting up, he put on his helmet and turned on the radios.
"Lead?"

"Go."

"Trail's up."

"Roger, Trail. What's it look like back there?"

Anderson surveyed the other aircraft. All had their rotating beacons on, which meant all were either up and running or were in the process of starting.

"You'll be up in about zero one."

"Roger that."

The grunts moved out of the shadows, toward the helicopters, climbing into them. Anderson watched four men get into the rear of his. Two of them sat on the troopseat with the two who were already there, and the other two sat on the deck.

"Flight, give a commo check in chock order."

"Two, roger."

"Three, roger."

"Four, roger."

"And Trail is up. You're loaded with five."

"Roger loaded. Coming up to a hover."

On the intercom, Nowlin asked, "Is this trip really necessary?"

"Of course not," said Anderson. "That's what makes it so much fun."

Lead picked up to a hover. The nav lights were on dim flash, and the rotating beacon had been turned off. Lead hung there for a moment as if examining the flight and then turned, facing away from them.

"Lead's on the go."

Anderson checked the instruments quickly and then saw the clock sitting on the far side of the instrument panel. It was coming up on one in the morning. Anderson was surprised by the time. He'd thought that it would be much later than that. He'd thought that daylight wasn't more than an hour away, but he saw that he was wrong.

The helicopters took off one by one, with more space left between them than normal. The pilots weren't used to flying at night, and no one wanted to fly into someone else. Anderson waited until each of the aircraft in front of him had crossed the bunker line before lifting up and dropping his chopper's nose.

As he did that, he said, "Lead, you're off with all five aircraft."

"Roger. Five Nine, say status."

"Five Nine is up but low on ammo. Six One is with me with a full load."

"Roger that."

Lead turned to the east but only climbed to a thousand feet. Anderson watched as the flight joined and then made the call. Lead rolled it over.

Anderson was searching the ground below them, watching the instruments, and trying to maintain his place in the formation. The Ho Bo Woods appeared as a large dark smudge on the ground to the right. There were patches of silver which were rice paddies reflecting the moonlight and starlight or the illumination of flares.

"You see anything?" he asked.

Nowlin touched the floor button. "Nothing."

They orbited outward from the camp. In the distance Anderson could make out the dull glow of the base at Cu

Chi and beyond that the brighter glow of Saigon. Directly below him it was almost pitch black. No individual lights. No security lights. Nothing but darkness.

"We're never going to find anything," said Nowlin. "This is a waste of time."

"You have something more important to do?" asked Anderson.

"I could be asleep."

"Here you are, participating in the great adventure. You are a soldier flying in harm's way. Movies are made about you. Books are written and stories are told. The warrior tradition has been handed down since before history was recorded, and all you want to do is go to sleep. Is that the way heroes are made?"

"Who wants to be a hero?" asked Nowlin.

"You say that now, but what about twenty years from now? You'll be sitting home, fat, telling the kids about the war. Do you want to have to say, well, I was there, but I went to sleep? Is that really what you want?"

"I just want the opportunity to say that," said Nowlin. "Besides, with the press the way it is, I probably won't want to tell anyone that I was even here. It'll be a secret, like a stay in the state pen."

"Thank you," said Anderson, "for making our ordeal here in South Vietnam into something common and derogatory. Thank you for turning the great adventure into the great secret that no one will talk about."

"You believe that crap you're always spouting?" asked Nowlin.

"Hell, no," said Anderson. "I'm just making noise so that I can stay awake."

"I thought so," said Nowlin. "You think we're going to find the enemy?"

"Of course," said Anderson.

"Why?"

"If you look out to the right, you'll see a line of tracers. Charlie's firing at us."

"What?"

Anderson keyed the mike for the radio. "Lead, we're taking fire on the right."

"Lead. Roger. We'll be turning in that direction. Let's get ready."

Anderson checked the instruments, turned down the lights, and flipped the lock on the inertia reel. Over the intercom, he said, "Brolin, get the grunts ready. Tell them we're heading in now."

"Roger."

Nowlin sat up straight, staring out the windshield. He was watching for more firing from the ground. "Damn, I don't want to do this."

"Look at the bright side," said Anderson. "It's night and they can't see us."

"They can see our lights."

"Right. Shut them off. We're the trail, and we don't need to have our lights on."

"Right."

Over the radio, Lead said, "I have an LZ in sight. Five Nine, are you ready?"

"Roger."

"Then here we go."

Anderson wanted to say something but didn't know what it should be. He hoped there was only one smart ass on the ground with a weapon and not an NVA company trying to draw them closer.

"Everyone get ready," he said unnecessarily. And then he wished that he'd kept his mouth shut and left Elway hiding in the bunker. He should have just joined him in there and not said a word.

# SIXTEEN

THE first rounds came up from the right—a single line of five or six green tracers. They missed the flight by a hundred yards or more. The muzzle flash was lost in the foliage of the Ho Bo Woods.

Anderson keyed the mike and said, "Flight's taking fire on the right."

"I've got it in sight," said Nichols. "Rolling in."

"Flaring," said Elway in Lead.

Anderson had just crossed the dark edge of the tree line. He touched the landing light, letting it stab out, showing him that the ground was rough and that there were saplings standing like the blades of grass on a newly germinated lawn.

Nichols rolled in, the minigun firing in short bursts. Tracers flashed down, disappearing into the trees. There was answering fire, heavier than before, a half-dozen weapons shooting back at the gunship.

Anderson leveled the skids and they touched down. As they did, the grunts leaped from the rear. Anderson used the radio. "Down and unloaded."

"On the go."

Lead picked up to a hover and then began a slow climb out designed to keep him from flying into the trees that surrounded the LZ. As he disappeared, the forest around the flight erupted. Chock Two took hits all along the right side of the aircraft. It rolled to the right and then fell, landing on its side. The rotors exploded into splinters as they slammed into the ground.

"Flight's taking heavy fire," said Anderson. "Chock Two is down in the LZ."

Three lifted to a high hover, dumped his nose, and began to get out. There was some firing at him. The door guns hammered, the muzzle flash strobing out three or four feet, lighting the side of the aircraft.

Chock Four did the same thing but then broke to the left. His door guns didn't fire. Anderson came up to a hover, dumped the chopper's nose, and headed toward the downed helicopter. He could see some of the crew getting out of it.

As he did, he hit the radio again. "Lead, you're out with three so far. I'm trying to get the downed crew."

"Roger. We'll hang close."

Anderson flared and touched the ground near the wreckage of Chock Two. As he did, the entire forest came alive. A hundred AKs opened fire. Tracers thicker than flies crisscrossed above him making it look as if the landing zone were under a glowing emerald net.

Now the GIs got into it, M-16s and M-60s firing. Red tracers flashed out. The muzzles of the weapons lit up the ground with the jerky light of an old movie. Men were moving around in a series of stop-action motions.

Anderson could hear rounds striking the helicopter. He could feel the damage being done to it. The door gunner was firing now, trying to stop the enemy—trying to force Charlie to keep his head down—but there were too many of them.

A round snapped through the windshield. A second followed the first. The instrument panel began to disintegrate and the turbine began to howl like a wounded animal. The EGT went sky-high and then the engine died.

"Lead, Trail's down in the LZ."

"Roger. We're coming around."

"Negative, Lead. Wait."

The crew from Chock Two was up and running toward them. Anderson grabbed the handle by his seat and popped the door. It fell from the aircraft, landing in the LZ. He stripped his helmet off and ordered, "Everyone out."

Grabbing the M-16 he had hung over the rear of his seat, Anderson dived from the cockpit. He fell to his knees and was suddenly aware of all the noise around him. Weapons firing on full auto. Men screaming in rage or pain. Bullets snapping by overhead. The pop of rotorblades and the roar of turbines in the distance.

"Nowlin?"

"Here."

"You zero the control heads?"

"You didn't say anything about that."

Anderson nodded and crawled back toward the aircraft. Bullets were still slamming into it, rocking it on the skids.

He could hear fuel bubbling from the ruptured cells. Keeping low, he reached up on the console and turned all the radio dials to zero. If they should lose the LZ and Charlie captured the downed helicopter before they could destroy it, he didn't want the enemy to know what frequencies they had been using.

He turned and dived back out. He crawled along the ground. The grunts had spread out and were pumping rounds back into the woods. The forest was alive with the enemy. The strobing from weapon muzzles sparkled everywhere.

Anderson moved past Nowlin, toward the first helicopter. He saw Clarke crouched near the cockpit, looking over the helicopter, into the woods.

"You okay?"

"Yeah, You?"

"Fine." Anderson turned around and sat with his back to the bottom of the helicopter, which lay on its side. He had never realized how loud the firefights could be. Everyone was firing as fast as possible. This was worse than the rifle range in basic, but there everyone had been firing on semiauto and he had been wearing earplugs.

Anderson pulled out his survival radio, yanked out the antenna, and said, "Lead, this is Trail."

"Go."

"We're down but safe. Heavy firing."

"Roger. We're not going to be able to get in there to get you out."

"Roger." That wasn't what he wanted to hear.

Almost from the moment they touched down, Morris knew they were in trouble. One guy brave enough to fire at a flight of helicopters probably meant more of them. As soon as the firing started, he knew the Americans were facing a company or more.

He tried to get the men off the choppers and down on the ground. He wanted the choppers to get off the LZ, but that didn't happen. Charlie was swarming through the trees, firing his weapons.

"Davis? Where are you?"

"Here."

Morris turned and found the lieutenant lying on the ground. He was not shooting.

"Get a squad together and go protect the downed pilots," Morris said.

There was a slight hesitation, and then Davis began to crawl away.

Morris turned and saw one of the sergeants. "Where in hell is the RTO?"

"Wounded. Radio took a number of hits. Saved the man's life."

"We got another one?"

"That was it, sir."

"Shit."

Morris watched as tracers flashed overhead. That was the thing about shooting at night. Everyone tended to shoot high. He got up, bent at the waist, and ran along the line. He leaped over a log that was little more than a black shape in the grass. Two men, one with an M-60 and the other with an M-79, lay there not moving.

Morris dropped beside them. "You men hurt?"

"No, sir."

"Let's put some rounds out."

"That'll just draw fire down on us."

"We lay here and don't do a thing, we're all going to die. Put out some rounds." Morris lifted himself slightly and then dropped back down. "Aim at the center of the muzzle flashes. Short bursts."

"Yes, sir."

Morris left the men and ran along the line. His men were slowly getting into the firefight. The shooting from them was sporadic but increasing. Ruby-red tracers were slamming into the woods.

"Grenades," called Morris. "Use grenades."

M-79s began blooping out their rounds, the grenades detonating in the woods. Flashes of sparks mushroomed, silhouetting the trees and sometimes enemy soldiers.

He reached the downed helicopters and found one of the pilots sitting there, a radio in his hand. "Is that thing working?"

"Yeah."

"Can you get us some artillery?"

"Where's your radio?"

"Shot to shit. We only had the one." Morris shook his head. "No one was thinking as we jumped on the choppers."

Anderson jerked out the antenna and then said, "Where do you want it?"

"In the woods there, where the enemy is."

"Blackhawk Lead, this is Three Séven. Can you get us some artillery support?"

"Roger," said Lead. "Where do you want it?"

"In the woods to the south."

"This is a guard frequency," said an unidentified voice. "It is to be used only in emergencies."

Anderson shot a glance at Morris and then said, "We are

down in a landing zone with the entire North Vietnamese Army about to overrun our position. That a big enough emergency for you, asshole?''

There was a hesitation, and then: "Can I be of assistance?"

"Negative. Blackhawk Lead?"

"Artillery coming in now."

"Roger."

Morris nodded and said, "I'm going to check on my men." He moved off and reached the end of the line, which had bent around so that the enemy couldn't outflank them. A staff sergeant was lying in the grass, directing the fire of a machine gun supported by both M-16s and M-79s.

Morris could see nothing wrong with the placement. The sergeant had done a good job. He crawled closer to the men, and said, "Artillery is coming in."

"We're ready, sir."

"You need any help, you sing out."

"Yes, sir."

Morris turned around again and surveyed the LZ. His troops were down, they had a defensive perimeter established, and they were putting out rounds. The enemy didn't seem inclined to leave the safety of the trees, and he was firing high. For the moment, everything seemed to be fine. At first light, they could get some choppers in and then get the hell out of there. All they had to do was hang on until first light.

Just as Anderson heard the first rush of an artillery shell, the Vietcong made their assault. The woods were full of bugles, whistles, and shouts. The firing increased as the enemy surged from the trees, dozens of small shapes that were little more than black smudges against the charcoal background of the forest.

Firing erupted all along the line. M-16s and M-60s poured fire into the attacking enemy. There were screams of hatred as the VC and NVA tried to overrun the American position.

Anderson tossed away his radio and turned to face the oncoming enemy. Using his M-16, he fired into the mass charging him. He pulled the trigger twice and realized that he couldn't fire fast enough. He flipped the selector to auto and began to fire four-and five-round bursts. In the dark it was impossible to use the metal sights. All he could do was look over the top of the weapon and try to keep his shots low.

As he fired, he saw some of the attacking shapes stumble and fall. All of the attackers were shooting their AKs. The muzzle flashes illuminated them. Rounds snapped over Anderson's head or ripped into the thin metal of the helicopter's tail boom.

Anderson was no longer aware of the men around him. His attention was focused on the attacking VC. They were the horror that could overwhelm him and kill him. He felt fear bubble in his belly, but he didn't stop firing. He kept at it until his weapon was empty. Then, dropping down, he jerked the spent magazine free, slammed a fresh one home, charged the weapon, and popped up again.

The enemy was closer to him. The soldiers were larger now—a jerking, flashing mass rushing forward. Anderson fired into it, short bursts at the closest of the enemy soldiers. Men were falling and screaming.

A single VC reached the aircraft and began to scramble over the tail boom. Anderson looked into the VC's dark, sweat-smeared face and pulled the trigger of his weapon.

The enemy was lifted from his perch and tossed back, screaming.

Another took his place, firing down toward Anderson. Everything slowed then, and Anderson was strangely calm. He turned toward the threat, grinned up at the enemy, and shot him in the face. Something hot and wet splashed him as the man fell off the helicopter.

A third ran around the end of the tail boom, and Anderson whirled to meet that threat. Before he could fire, the man was hit half a dozen times. Two Americans, firing on full auto, turned on him and cut him down. He threw his weapon up, into the air, as he dropped into the grass.

Now Anderson saw the others around him—dark shapes crouching in the grass, behind the wrecked helicopters, behind logs or bushes, or lying in the grass, firing at the enemy soldiers. Muzzle flashes reached out, three-and four-foot-long spurts of flame, and touched the enemy. Tracers streaked and bounced. Some hit the onrushing black shapes. Small fires burned in the grass where the muzzle flashes or the tracers had touched it.

Cries of anguish filled the night. A man called, "Medic! Medic!" over and over. Another just screamed, his words unintelligible.

Anderson moved along the tail boom, back toward the tail rotor. He crouched in the grass, and aimed over the aircraft. He hesitated for a moment, knowing that his muzzle flash would give him away. But then he realized that he had to fire. Everyone had to fire, or the enemy would quickly overrun them.

He fired again. Once, twice. Behind the attackers, the woods were blowing up. Artillery rounds were crashing into the trees back there—bright flashes of red-orange fire.

Then, as suddenly as they had come, the enemy soldiers began to retreat. They fled from the field, turning their backs, halting their fire. From the trees, the RPDs continued to shoot, covering the retreat.

Anderson dropped down, behind the protective cover of the tail boom. He felt a round smash into it—heard the metal tear. And then the enemy was gone.

Firing became sporadic as the Americans tried to keep the VC and the NVA from attacking again. Anderson turned and crawled back toward the cargo compartment of the downed aircraft. He found one body, a VC, lying near it. He stood up and stepped over it. Lying facedown in the grass was Clarke. Anderson knelt but could find no pulse.

Then he heard the insectile buzz of the survival radio. He searched the grass for it, finally found it, and lifted it to his ear.

"What's going on down there? Come in, anyone. What is happening down there?"

Anderson wiped his face on the sleeve of his jungle fatigues. He keyed the mike and said, "This is Three Seven."

"Three Seven, this is Lead. What's going on?"

"We had some trouble." As he spoke, Anderson realized that the artillery had stopped firing. Almost everyone had stopped firing. A few rounds, M-16 going out and AK coming in, snapped overhead—sniping by both sides.

"We were attacked by the enemy but have beaten them back. Three Two is dead. I don't know about the others."

There was a long silence and then, "Say status."

Anderson realized that it was a stupid question. Elway

had to know the status. Two aircraft down in the LZ, at least one pilot dead, and the enemy all around them.

"We're going to need help," said Anderson. "Medevac and resupply. And artillery support. We're going to need that artillery. And tell Five Nine we're going to need everything he can put in the back of a gunship."

"Roger. Hang on. We're working on it."

Anderson didn't say anything. There was nothing that he could say.

# SEVENTEEN

**M**ORRIS moved along the line slowly, checking his soldiers, making sure they had all the ammo they would need, checking their morale, and giving them a few words of encouragement where they were needed. It was all he could do. With the VC and NVA swarming in the woods, with the LZ now choked with the wreckage of the downed aircraft, and with the sun still a couple of hours away, he couldn't do anything else. Words of hope and ammo were all that he had.

"Sir," said one of the sergeants, crawling over to him. "We've taken quite a few casualties."

"You get a count?"

"Not a good one. I make it fifteen dead and twelve wounded. About two-thirds of the force."

"How bad are the wounded?"

"A couple are going to have to be evacced or they're not going to make it. One guy took a bullet through the head, and I don't know how the hell it didn't kill him."

Morris pushed on, working his way up to the first helicopter. He found Anderson sitting with his back to the bottom of the chopper, the radio clutched in his hand.

"How goes it?"

"I'm ready," said Anderson. "Clarke's dead." He nodded toward the body.

Morris wondered if Clarke had been counted as one of the fifteen dead. He asked, "Can we get a medevac in here sometime soon?"

"I don't think so," said Anderson. "Not with the enemy as thick as they are. It'd be shot down before it could get close enough to land."

"We've got some badly wounded..."

"Daylight?" said Anderson.

Morris pulled at the sleeve of his jungle fatigues and then lifted his wrist close to his eyes. "Couple of hours yet. Too long."

"We can try," said Anderson. "But I don't think the helicopter will be able to make it."

"Arrange it," said Morris.

He moved off, working his way to the end of the line. The machine gun was still there, but now it was a twisted wreck. A grenade had gone off near it, bending the barrel back and smashing the trigger housing and the breech. One man lay dead near it. Another, his hand wrapped in a bandage, was crouched there, a grenade launcher and an M-16 near him. His face was pale, easily visible in the darkness.

"We did the best we could," he said.

"Hang on," said Morris. "The choppers are on the way back in."

"Yes, sir."

As he turned, the woods were suddenly alive with the enemy. They swarmed out, screaming and shouting. There was a moment's hesitation and then the line began to fire—full auto, immediately. Grenades detonated as the enemy surged across the open ground.

Morris was on his knees, yelling, "Open fire! Open fire!" He jerked at the trigger of his own weapon, held it down, and burned through the whole twenty-round magazine.

Anderson jumped up as the new attack began. He watched the enemy come at him and then dropped down. Over the radio, he said, "They're coming again. Out of the trees."

"Roger," said Elway.

That was not the response that Anderson wanted. Keying the mike, he asked, "Where are the guns?"

"Ah, Three Seven, this is Five Nine."

"Five Nine, they're coming at us from the south. Can you put it on them?"

"Where are you?"

"About halfway between the trees on either side of the LZ. Make your run from west to east and hit the trees on the south. Right on the edge."

"Roger that."

Anderson set the radio down, next to the bottom of the helicopter, and picked up his M-16. He popped up and fired over the top of the chopper.

As he did, Nichols began the first of the gun runs. The red ray from the miniguns reached out and danced along the edge of the tree line. The roar of the weapon drowned out all other sound. The ground erupted. Branches from the trees fell. Trunks exploded under the impact of the rounds.

From deeper in the woods came the deep-throated chug of .51-caliber machine guns—first one, then two, and finally a half-dozen of them. The huge, basketball-sized, green-glowing tracers loomed upward.

Nichols broke the gun run and turned north, over the LZ and away from the enemy. The second ship rolled in. The enemy turned a hundred AKs on it. The attack sputtered as the enemy fought to get back into the safety of the trees, but now they were firing up, at the helicopters. Tracers flashed skyward like a huge Fourth of July display.

The gunship was forced to break the attack. It turned to the north just as Nichols rolled in again. The minigun fired short bursts into the trees. The enemy soldiers responded, trying to knock their attacker from the sky.

Anderson picked up the radio. "Five Nine. Five Nine. They've broken the assault."

The gunship turned and Anderson heard, "Roger, Three Seven. We're about out of ammo."

"Roger."

Anderson was leaning across the rear of the helicopter, his M-16 in his hand. The tree line was sparkling as the enemy force turned its weapons on the Americans in the LZ. Rounds snapped overhead. A few grenades exploded—weak things that had almost no bursting power and very little shrapnel.

Anderson fired a couple of shots and then dropped back to the ground. As he lifted the radio, Morris loomed out of the darkness.

"We're getting cut to pieces."

"There's nothing I can do about it. You saw the intense fire at the guns."

"We need an air strike. We need artillery."

Anderson knew that Morris was right. They had to do something or they were going to be overwhelmed. Charlie smelled the victory and he wasn't about to let go of it. At least not easily.

Anderson lifted the radio, "Blackhawk Four Six, this is Three Seven."

"Go."

"Can you get an air strike in here?"

There was a moment's hesitation and then, "I can try. Might be a while."

Anderson looked at Morris. "He'll try."

"Somebody better do something or we're not going to make it until morning."

Anderson nodded and used the radio again. "Four Six, can you lay on artillery? Into the woods south of here. That's where the enemy is now. Lay it right in there."

"Roger."

After a short wait, Lead said, "We have the rounds on the way."

An instant later there was a loud rushing sound followed by a sudden crash. Anderson didn't see where the round had landed but didn't care. Over the radio, he shouted, "Keep it coming. Keep it coming."

Before Morris could move, the enemy attacked again. The soldiers made no noise this time. They surged from the trees, running as fast as they could, trying to overrun the defenders before they could open fire.

"Here they come!" yelled a man.

Firing erupted, but this time it was too late. The enemy was too close. Morris stood to meet the onrushing figures and a VC hurled himself at the American. Morris sidestepped and punched. The VC fell to the ground. Morris whirled and shot him once in the back.

The fighting was now hand to hand. Morris used his M-16, swinging the stock around to hit another enemy. There wasn't much force behind the blow. Morris lost his grip on the weapon and dropped it. He stepped close, and grabbed the barrel of the AK, jerking it forward. He slammed his elbow into the man's face, hearing and feeling the bones snap. As the man staggered back, Morris jerked the AK from his hands, reversed it, and fired once, into the man's chest.

Morris used the AK then, firing into the attackers. One man went down. Then another. Morris stepped back and slipped to one knee.

"Medic!" yelled someone.

Morris turned toward the sound and saw two VC running at him. He fired from the hip. One of them died instantly. The other returned fire. The rounds snapped by Morris's head. He shot back and the man screamed as he died.

Anderson emptied his M-16 but didn't have time to reload it. There were too many VC too close to him. He dropped the weapon and drew his pistol. He fired at the closest of the enemy soldiers. The man shouted as if in pain but kept right on coming. Anderson fired again and again, sure that he was hitting the enemy. As he reached Anderson, the enemy soldier staggered and slipped to his knees. Anderson stepped up and kicked, catching the man in the chest, knocking him to the ground.

Anderson stepped to the rear and broke open the cylinder of his revolver. He dumped the spent shells from the chambers and then began to fumble with the bullets, trying to reload. Now he was aware of everything going on around him. Every sound, every motion, everything was etched into his mind. The odor of death hung over the LZ. Hot copper and human bowel. There were screams. Men in rage and men in pain. There were bugle calls and whistles and the hammering of machine guns and automatic rifles, all punctuated by grenades detonating, and behind all that roared the artillery.

Anderson realized that his pistol wasn't going to help. He threw it down and dropped to his hands and knees, searching for his M-16, a black shape concealed in the grass. He found a weapon, picked it up, and worked the bolt. Now he held an AK-47. He didn't care. He stood, found a target, and fired.

Tracers were thick over the LZ. Rounds were slamming into the aircraft and snapping past him. Anderson ducked down and picked up the radio. Someone was going to have to do something or they wouldn't survive until morning.

Keying it, Anderson yelled, "Four Six. Four Six. Put the artillery down on us."

"What?"

"We are being overrun. Bring the artillery down on our position."

"I can't do that," said Elway.

Anderson dropped down. He held the radio close to his lips. "It doesn't fucking matter. They're overrunning us now. We need that artillery."

"Roger." There was a hesitation and then, "Rounds on the way."

Anderson stood up and screamed, "Incoming. Artillery on the way. Take cover."

But the two sides were too mixed to separate. They fought with one another using knives and rifle butts and bare hands. They kicked and clawed and used their teeth. Desperate men, they used anything as a weapon, trying to kill the enemy as quickly as they could.

The first round hit near the trees on the south side of the LZ. There was a flash of bright light and then a concussion of hot air. Shrapnel whistled through the night. Anderson dropped flat, his hands over his head, and listened to the artillery falling around him.

Now the air was filled with cries of terror. Artillery was raining down on the LZ. The detonations overwhelmed the other sounds, and the odor of cordite eliminated everything else. The falling rounds made noise. Not the whistling of bombs from World War II movies, but a rumbling rush as they dropped. Some exploded in the air, throwing out shrapnel that shredded everything and everyone standing upright. Others exploded on the ground, tossing clouds of dirt upward. The concussions shook the ground.

The enemy began to flee in terror. They ran for the safety of the trees, breaking contact. They dropped their weapons in their panic. They knocked one another down and they left their wounded on the field.

Anderson tried to force himself into the ground. He wanted to become part of the terrain. He wanted to vanish so that the artillery wouldn't kill him. This was worse than the mortar and rocket attacks, because those had been small, almost ineffective weapons, and he had been hiding in a bunker. Artillery was larger and deadlier. He didn't understand how anything could live through an attack.

He clutched the radio in his right hand, lying on it as if to protect it. He could hear someone talking on it but couldn't make out the muffled words. He pulled it out.

"Three Seven. Three Seven. This is Lead."

"Go."

"Where have you been?"

There was a tremendous crash and dirt rained down on his back.

"What the hell was that?"

"Artillery," said Anderson. "You can call it off."

"Wait one." An instant later Elway was back. "Last rounds on the way."

"Roger," said Anderson. He waited for the last six artillery rounds, afraid that they would fall on him. He heard the rumble of them and then the blasts as they detonated.

"All rounds on the ground and tubes clear," said Elway.

"Roger. Stand by."

Morris ran up, his face streaked with dirt and sweat beading his forehead. He wiped at it and said, "You called that artillery in on us?"

Anderson didn't know what to say. He'd thought that it was the only thing that could save them but it had been a presumptuous thing to do. He hadn't been in command. It hadn't been his decision to make.

"I had to," he said.

Morris nodded. "I think it saved us. It was the only thing that could. Well done."

"Thanks."

"Now, if we can get out of here . . ."

Anderson nodded and then realized that he could clearly see Morris. The sun was coming up. He turned and looked back at the trees to the south. He could see them, and the bodies strewn between the woods and the American lines. Black smoke drifted on the light breeze.

"Sunrise," said Anderson.

"Damn," said Morris. "I think we've made it."

# EIGHTEEN

MORRIS wiped his face again and looked right at Anderson. "Can we get the hell out of here?"

"Yeah," said Anderson. "I think it's time." He lifted the radio. "Four Six, this is Three Seven."

"Go."

"We need to get out of here."

"Roger. We're getting another flight put together. ETA in about fifteen minutes."

Anderson looked at Morris. "Medevac?" he asked.

"We've got wounded that need to be evacked," said Anderson on the radio.

"Roger. Wait one."

Anderson rubbed his face. There was still sporadic firing. A machine gun fired a short burst and then a long one. An AK answered that. There was an explosion from a grenade.

"We can put one ship in."

"One ship," said Anderson.

"How many can it carry?"

"Six or seven. The ones hurt the worst."

"That should be enough," said Morris. He got up and ran toward the west.

"Let's get it in," said Anderson on the radio.

"Roger."

He set the radio down and then looked at the AK he held. He had no idea how many rounds were still in the magazine. He didn't have any way to reload it except to strip the VC bodies. Then he spotted the butt of his M-16. He picked it up and worked the bolt, but that did nothing. He pulled the magazine from the well, looked into it, and saw that it was empty. He turned the weapon around and saw that the barrel was clean. He pulled a new magazine from his bandolier, slammed it home, and worked the bolt again.

"Three Seven?"

Anderson picked up the radio. "Three Seven."

"Medevac is ready. Can you throw smoke?"

"Roger, if you really want it."

"Have the men ready to load. I don't want to stay on the ground any longer than I have to."

"Neither do I," said Anderson.

He stood up and looked back. The ground was still dark, but not like it had been. He could see the men crouched behind the low barricades they'd thrown up during the night. Logs had been dragged in. Some men had scraped at the ground with knives, digging out shallow fighting holes. One man lay behind the bodies of enemy soldiers killed in the fighting.

Holding the radio in one hand and his rifle in the other,

Anderson ran along the line. He found Morris kneeling near one of his badly wounded men. The man's chest was covered in blood, and there was a huge bandage tied in place. His face looked waxy and was sweat soaked.

"Medevac is coming in."

"When?"

"Now. We'll have to get the wounded gathered."

"Inbound," said the radio.

Anderson lifted the radio. "Roger. Throwing smoke." He glanced at Morris.

"Here. Close to here."

Anderson said, "Somebody throw a smoke grenade."

One of the men stood, pulled a pin, and tossed the grenade fifteen or twenty feet to the north of them. It popped, flamed, and began to billow smoke.

"ID yellow," said the radio.

"Roger, yellow." Anderson lowered the radio and said, "Let's get them ready. We keep them on the ground too long they're going to get shot to shit."

"I know," snapped Morris.

Anderson nodded. He turned at the distant sound of a helicopter. "Get ready."

He watched the aircraft approach from the west. It flew low, using the trees for cover. A single line of tracers reached up for it but missed. The chopper came over the tree line but didn't seem to be slowing. It dropped lower as the trees to the south erupted again, green tracers flashing.

The helicopter suddenly turned, up on its side, and its blades began to bite at the air. As it slowed abruptly, it righted and touched down.

The gunships rolled in, miniguns firing. Now there weren't short bursts. They were hosing down the trees. The enemy firing tapered off suddenly, as if Charlie was searching for cover.

The men were up and moving, carrying their wounded friends toward the helicopter. Over the roar of the turbine and the popping of the rotors, Anderson could hear someone yelling, "Hurry it up. Hurry."

Anderson watched as the rest of the men on the ground began to fire at the trees. He could see movement in there now, but didn't know if it was the result of the minigun rounds ripping the forest apart, or if it was the enemy running. Anderson lowered his weapon and opened fire.

The sound behind him changed, and there was a hurricane wind from the rotorwash. The helicopter stayed low, gaining speed. It popped up suddenly, lifted over the trees, and disappeared.

When it was gone, the firing tapered off slowly until it was only sporadic. Morris came to him and said, "Looks like they're bugging out."

"Yeah, but I'd like to get out of here myself," said Anderson.

"What about Eagle Eye?" Morris was grinning.

"Fuck Eagle Eye right now." Anderson hesitated and then said, "I've got to see about the others. I'm missing six men."

"We put a pilot on the medevac chopper," said Morris.

"Christ. Who?"

"I don't know. He was hit in the stomach and leg. Lost a lot of blood but wasn't in real danger yet."

Anderson shook his head. He'd forgotten about the other flight crews. He knew that Clarke was dead. But he hadn't seen Nowlin or Jameson or Brolin since they had been shot down. He began to move along the line, searching for his friends.

At the remains of his aircraft, he found Brolin's body. The crew chief had been shot four or five times. His uniform was rust colored, stained by his blood.

Nowlin was under the nose of the helicopter lying on his stomach. He was using the toe of the skid for protection. He had both an M-16 and an AK. Anderson crouched near the cross tube. "You doing okay, Dan?"

Nowlin turned and looked back. "I just want to get the hell out. I never planned on being in the infantry."

"Well, maybe we'll get a Combat infantryman's Badge out of it."

"I'd rather have a beer and a steak."

As he knelt there, the radio crackled to life again. "Blackhawk Three Seven, this is Blackhawk Six."

Anderson felt his stomach turn over. With Six in the area, could the flight be far behind? "This is Three Seven."

"The flight is inbound your location."

"Roger." Anderson wanted to say more but didn't know what it could be. He waited.

"Say condition of LZ."

"We still have some VC and NVA in the trees. They are armed with automatic weapons, including some .51-cals. There are two aircraft down in the LZ, but we won't need more than five aircraft to get out."

"Roger that. We'll be ready to make the extraction in five minutes. Be ready."

"Roger that." Anderson stared at Nowlin's back. "You hear that?"

Nowlin slipped backward and then rolled out from under the nose of the helicopter. "I'm ready."

"Pass the word to the east and get the other flight crews together. Clarke is dead and I think Jameson has been evacked. Brolin is dead too."

"I saw him get it," said Nowlin.

Anderson shook his head. "I don't think I want to hear about it now."

Nowlin, carrying his weapon and crouched low like the infantrymen in a hundred war movies, ran toward the east, telling the soldiers that more helicopters were on the way.

Anderson headed back toward Morris. "We need to get the men ready to extract."

"Dead?"

"Everyone. I think they'll use the guns to blow up the downed aircraft. This whole place is going to blow up in a few minutes."

"Souvenirs?" asked Morris.

"Who the fuck cares about souvenirs?"

"Can the men carry extra weapons?"

"Yeah. That shouldn't be a problem."

Again the radio crackled. "Three Seven. Guns are going to make a run first. See what they draw in the way of fire."

"Roger that." Anderson looked at Morris. "Let's get the men ready."

"We're ready now."

Anderson keyed the mike. "Six, this is Three Seven. We're ready to go."

"Guns coming in now."

The first of them opened fire with rockets. One pair. Two. Three. Four. They slammed into the trees, exploding there, throwing out shrapnel. The aircraft broke to the north, away form the old enemy positions, and the next gunship rolled in with its miniguns firing.

"We have you in sight," said Lead's pilot.

Firing broke out in the woods. Some of the tracers came at Anderson, but others were sent up, at the gunships and then the slicks. The door guns joined in now—five more machine guns pouring fire into the trees.

Anderson ran to the front of the LZ and held his weapon over his head as he'd see grunts do in the past. They had joked about John Wayne, but Anderson wanted Lead to know exactly where to touch down. He heard the rounds snap by his head, but ignored them.

He watched as the first of the slicks flared over the tops of the trees. He could see the bottoms of the aircraft clearly now. It was a view of the Huey that he'd never had. He could see that messages had been painted on the bottoms of a couple of them. He hadn't known that was done. One said, "Death from above." Another said, simply, "Here we come."

The firing grew in intensity, and he prayed that the ships would land and then knew they would. He'd never been involved in a go-around with troops on the ground. He knew that the pilots would land as Charlie filled their Plexiglas world with lead, because he'd done it himself.

As the lead aircraft approached, Anderson dived to the right and rolled out of the way. He suddenly had a new appreciation for the pilots. He'd always felt bad about dropping the grunts off in a hot LZ and then flying away. He'd often wondered if they hated the pilots because they could get out. He knew, in that moment, that the grunts respected them for doing what they had to do—come in, land, and get out. Maybe they got to fly to comfort in the evening, but it was those few seconds when they came in to pick up the grunts that made all the difference.

Lead touched down and Anderson was up and running. He stepped up on the skid and reached out, grabbing at the back of an armored seat to pull himself up and in. As he scrambled out of the way, a body was dumped in behind him. He could smell the odor of hot copper over those of metal and jet fuel and the scorched earth of the LZ.

Another man appeared, and Anderson reached out, grabbing him, hauling him in. The man smiled up at him. "Thanks."

In seconds the chopper was loaded and the door gun was firing, the brass falling out, into the LZ. Anderson glanced at the cockpit as a round snapped through the windshield. Neither pilot flinched.

"Let's go," he yelled.

And then they picked up to a hover. Anderson understood that Trail had just cleared him. Anderson had never known what it was like to sit in the back of a chopper while the enemy fired at you, and the pilots seemed to be frozen at the controls. He hadn't realized the terror of it because he had always been up front, flying. He'd had something to do, and he had controlled his own destiny. Now it belonged to the pilot in front of him. It was a frightening feeling.

The nose dropped and they began to race for the far tree line. Outside, through the cargo-compartment door, Anderson could see the remains of one of the downed helicopters. It was on its side, and the enemy was shooting at it again as if making sure that it would never get out. Flames began to lick at it, and suddenly it shuddered and exploded. Flaming debris scattered, setting fires all around the LZ. There would be nothing of value left for the enemy to exploit.

Anderson watched the scene disappear as they crossed the

top of the tree line. The door guns fell silent, and Anderson realized that they were clear. He had survived.

He glanced at the faces of the men with him, knowing that the majority of them were only nineteen or twenty years old. No older than he was. Kids who should have been seniors in high school or freshmen in college. Kids who had no business fighting in a real war.

And then he looked at the face of the dead man. A blood-stained face, the eyes closed but the mouth open. Another kid who wouldn't have the chance to go to college and chase the cheerleaders.

And finally, he was happy. He had gotten out when it had looked as if he was going to die. He had survived Eagle Eye. He had survived his own big mouth.

"Christ," he yelled over the roar of the turbine and the pop of the rotors.

One of the grunts looked at him and held up a thumb. That said it all.

# NINETEEN

ANDERSON and Nichols were sitting in the Gunfighter's Club in the middle of the afternoon. The jukebox was playing, but the music was soft, turned down so that the men and the few women there could talk to one another without having to shout. There was no one dancing on the stage and no one scheduled to dance for two hours.

Sitting in front of the two pilots were the empty beer bottles. They had refused to let the waitress take them away. It was the way they were keeping track of exactly how much they'd had to drink. Sitting in front of the empty chairs were full bottles. Those were for the friends who hadn't survived The Night of the Eagle Eye. That was the name Anderson had given it.

"Can't believe that Morris wants to put you in for a

medal," said Nichols. "Can't believe that he thinks you're the bravest man who ever lived. What an asshole. Calling the artillery in on yourself."

"Can't believe that Morris wants to put you in for a medal," said Anderson. "You fire a few bullets into the Ho Bo Woods and he thinks you're the bravest man who ever flew."

"If you hadn't gotten your ass shot out of the sky, he'd have thought that of you," said Nichols.

"All I want," said Anderson, "is a damned CIB. Grunts can get the Distinguished Flying Cross and the Air Medal, why can't I have a Combat Infantryman's Badge?"

"What'd he say?"

"You have to be assigned to an infantry unit in combat for thirty days. I think they do that to keep the rest of us from getting them."

"That's the way it goes," said Nichols. He took a drink from his beer. "Guess they'll cancel Eagle Eye now."

"Why do you say that?"

"Well we went out and got shot to shit. They'll cancel it because of the casualties."

Anderson nodded. "I suppose you're right, if they look at it only from that point of view. There were what, two pilots killed and one crew chief. Of course, I hear that the grunts found over two hundred dead in the woods. They swept through as fast as they could. There might have been more that the enemy carried away. More that we'll never know about."

"Not to mention the grunts killed."

"Of course," said Anderson. "Although they lost seventeen or eighteen. We're still way ahead. It's a kill ratio of better than ten to one."

"They won't look at it that way," said Nichols, finishing his beer.

"But that's what it all boils down to, and the kill ratio would be higher if we hadn't run into that reinforced battalion. Hell, Eagle Eye works. We go out three times and we catch the enemy all three times. Until we stop finding the enemy, they should keep Eagle Eye going."

Nichols signaled for the waitress and then said, "I think it's like the two-minute drill in football."

"What?"

"Haven't you ever wondered why, if a team can move the ball during the last two minutes, if they can change their plan for the last two minutes and make it down the field, why they don't play the whole game that way?"

Anderson nodded. "Okay, I'll bite. Why?"

"Intensity. You can't have your team playing at that intensity for the full game. You'd burn them out quickly."

The waitress appeared, looked at them, and then retreated without a word. She knew they wanted more beer.

"So," said Anderson, "you're telling me that Eagle Eye is too intense."

"Exactly."

"But isn't that the way you should fight a war? Intense? Push the enemy at every chance, keep at him until he can take it no more?"

"Sure," said Nichols, nodding, "if you want to win."

"Then we're right back at the beginning. Our side is content to make contact once in a while to let the war sort of happen. Eagle Eye forces it to happen."

"Exactly," said Nichols again. "That's why they're going to cancel it, though they'll blame it on the casualties. Don't want to sacrifice young lives needlessly."

The beer arrived, and the waitress collected the money and left again.

"Well, I'm thankful for that attitude, but if they were really worried about young lives, they'd never have gotten us involved in this mess in the first place."

"I'd have to agree with that," said Nichols. He picked up his new beer and took a sip. He pointed with the bottom of the bottle and asked, "That your friend?"

Anderson turned and saw Sandy walk into the club. "Yeah," he said, standing.

She spotted him and moved toward him rapidly. She pulled out a chair and sat down. "Looks like you two have been busy," she said.

"Been here for an hour or so," he said.

"You didn't call."

"Nope. I figured that you'd be working."

She picked up his beer and drank from it. As she set it down, she said, "Thanks. I needed that."

Nichols said, "I suddenly feel like a fifth wheel."

Anderson turned to him and then looked back at Sandy. "I don't have to be back for a couple of days."

"Really?" she said.

"Got the time off after flying so much in the last week. Way over on flight time. The CO told me to head to Saigon and take a couple of days off."

"Really?" she repeated.

"Said to relax. Ordered me not to think about flying for a couple of days."

"Uh-huh," she said. "Do you have a plan for all this time off?"

"Well, I hadn't really thought of anything beyond drinking a few beers with my friend here, but I've already done that. My plans don't extend beyond that."

She reached out and took his hand. "If you're not glued to that chair, I have an idea."

"I had hoped you would."

"Then let's get out of here," she said.

Anderson stood up and looked at Nichols. "You'll find some way to entertain yourself?"

"I think so," said Nichols. "You have something to do?"

Anderson glanced at Sandy, who was grinning slyly. "Yeah," said Anderson. "I think we can find something to do."